PICKET LINE BLUES

Prelude to a Riot

a novel by

Nino E. Green

This book is a work of fiction. Characters, and their names are products of the author's imagination or are used fictitiously. All rights are reserved and no part of this book may be reproduced in whole or in part without written permission from the author except by reviewers who may quote brief excerpts in a review in a newspaper, magazine or electronic publication. No part of this book may be reproduced, stored in a retrieval system or transmitted in any form or by any means electronic, mechanical, photocopying, recording or any other means, without written permission from the author.

About the author:

A 1963 graduate of Wayne Law School, Nino began his career in Detroit in 1964 and practiced law in the courts of Wayne, Oakland, Macomb, and several other lower Michigan counties and the United States District Court for the Eastern District of Michigan. He left Detroit in 1966 to become the first executive director of Upper Peninsula Legal Services, a position that he held for two and one half years. In 1969, he entered the private practice of law at Escanaba, and in 1976, he became the senior partner in the Upper Peninsula law firm of Green, Renner, Weisse, Rettig, Rademacher and Clark.

Green has practiced in the Upper Peninsula's probate district and circuit courts, the United States District Courts for the Western District of Michigan, the Michigan Court of Appeals, Michigan Supreme Court, and the U.S. Sixth and Eighth Circuit Courts of Appeals. He is a 2003 recipient of the John W. Commisky Pro Bono award, he has been recognized by the Legal Services Corporation for his work on behalf of indigent clients. He has been a member of the Mackinac Island State Park Commission, and the Michigan Employment Relations Commission. He is a former Chairperson of Legal Services of Northern Michigan.

Acknowledgements

Dedicated to the memory of Connie Osier who encouraged me to tell this story and to the union leaders, members and others who provided much of the narrative. A special thanks to my friends, Teresa Ross and Joan Rust, my wife,Chris Leonard-Green and my daughter, Leah Belanger, who gave generously of their time and saved me from the embarrassment of mistakes I would not have discovered.

Chapter One

The business manager of a local union of ironworkers hurried from the frigid darkness of a winter morning in International Falls, into the lighted warmth of Lulu's Cafe. He sat on one of several vinyl-covered stools at the counter, and snow began to drip from his hatless head. Pulling off a pair of fleece-lined gloves, he reached for a paper napkin and wiped the droplets from his brow. After shoving the gloves into a pocket of his Mackinaw, he turned the collar down and surveyed the diner while waiting for his coffee to be poured.

"You're the first one in," she announced. "What brings you here on such a miserable morning? It's freezing outside, but the coffee is fresh made and hot."

She was wearing her familiar blue slacks, pink blouse and tennis shoes. Her apron had freshly laundered stains. He watched her pour.

"I got into town yesterday afternoon for a meeting with the other building trades before we sat down with Boise-Cascade's mill management. When we were finished, some of us went to Benny's Saloon. I hadn't intended to stay very long .I wanted to get an early start this morning."

He checked his watch and added, "It's still early isn't it? I guess I didn't oversleep."

She set her coffeepot on the counter. "Is BoiseCascade about to do something that will give our little town a reason to celebrate?"

"Can't say. Nothing's final yet."\

"C'mon. Tell me. What happened at the meeting."

"Who said anything 'bout a meeting'?"

"You did."

"Well then, keep it to yourself."

"You mean you'll tell me?"

He shook his head. She pouted and went to the far end of the counter where she had been sitting before he came in. He watched her reach into her apron for a cigarette, light a match to it and take a long drag. He shook his head again and went back to his coffee.

Lulu's Cafe, tucked into a row of windowed storefronts, was

a fewshort blocks from Boise-Cascade's paper mill. In winter, morning comes late to International Fall and at 6:30, Lulu's large, plate glass window casts light onto a darkened sidewalk. Inside, the diner has a tin ceiling above a floor of black and white linoleum squares. Its formica counter guards the kitchen. Beyond a center row of tables there are red vinyl-booths and a mirrored wall that make the room appear much larger than it is. Before the arrival of Lulu's early-bird customers, mostly shift workers from the mill, the only sounds come from the kitchen where someone rattles pots and pans and opens and closes a refrigerator and cupboard doors.\\

Lulu's serves breakfast six-thirty to eleven-thirty, Monday through Saturday mornings, from a menu of standard fare: eggs with bacon, sausage or ham, corned beef hash or hash browns, toast or pancakes. From noon to six, it has homemade soup or chili, burgers and a variety of sandwiches with French fries, onion rings or slaw. Dinner choices are the same until closing time. Coffee, soft drinks, pastries and fresh-baked pie are available throughout the day.

Jack Ross' stomach growled as he sipped his coffee and studied the daily specials scrawled in uneven letters on a chalkboard behind the counter.

"Are you sure I can't get you something else?" the middle-aged waitress called to him from the far end of the counter.

"No thanks. Coffee is all. I'm trying to lose a few pounds."

"Good luck with that," she said.

After he left the ironworker trade to become his union's business manager, Jack added some weight to his once lean frame. He didn't want to admit toWanda that he was hungry. When Wanda refilled his cup, he lifted it, no cream, no sugar, and winced.

"Black and hot, hey?" she quipped, adding,"Just coffee, no breakfast and you're ready to go back to Duluth after one meeting."

"Two meetings if you count the one with the building trades. It was getting dark when we finished is why I checked into a motel and stayed the night. You can never tell what the weather's gonna be like this time of year. I hate driving through snow at night. Maybe the next time I come, the snow will be gone."

Wanda looked to be about the same age as his wife, but Wanda was taller and a bit heavier than Edith. There also was something brash about Wanda's dark, pencil-thin eyebrows and red lipstick. Edith didn't wear makeup. He couldn't tell what Wanda's breasts were like, but he imagined that they were small, like Edith's. He wanted to empty his cup and be on his way home before anyone else arrived. If they heard about the meeting, there would be questions. When his eyes caught sight of doughnuts in a glass display case next to the cash register by the window, he feigned a cough when his stomach growled again.

"You sure I can't get you something to eat?"

She set her coffeepot on the warming plate behind the counter and began wrapping flatware in paper napkins, setting them in a neat pile. Jack watched until someone came in with a gust of chilly air and took the stool next to him.

"'Mornin Wanda. Mornin' Jack. When did you drive up?"

Hank Peterson was a senior ironworker who attended most union meetings and never failed to vote in a union election.

"I got here yesterday."

"Stayed the night, hey?"

It ain't exactly camping weather. I checked into a motel. Soon as I'm done with my coffee, I'll-begone."

Wanda finished wrapping utensils and was flipping through a magazine. When Hank came in, she got up, grabbed her coffeepot, set a cup in front of him and filled it.

"Can I get you anything else?"

"I'll have one'a those." Hank pointed. "Make it a glazed."

They watched her go to the glass case, reach in and return with Hank's treat in a fold of waxed paper.

"How's Mary?" she asked.

"Same as always. No better, no worse. She was up most' of the night again, but she was asleep when I left."

Hank's wife was crippled with arthritis. Coffee at Lulu's was his morning respite while she slept after a restless night.

"I imagine she'll sleep 'til noon," he added.

He unwrapped the doughnut, breaking off a piece, dunking I and leaving the rest next to his coffee. Jack waited for him to offer to share. When he didn't, Jack asked for more coffee.

Hank's back was slightly bent and his gait was measured, but he had strong, sinewy arms and large rough hands. Although pension-eligible at the age of sixty-three, he wasn't thinking of retiring, but he had been without work since the late fall. Earlier in the winter, Jack offered him a referral to a short-term job in Des Moines.

"It's only for a couple of weeks, but it's easy work."

"Thanks, but I can get by on my unemployment checks, " Hank replied. "If I stay in town, I can look after Mary by myself. If I leave, I'd have to put her in a nursing home."

"When construction starts up in the spring, the first call to work will be yours," Jack assured him. "You've been on the bench longer than most."

"When construction starts up, I'll be ready to go back to work. It's been a long winter. Mary and me are beginning to get on each other's nerves. Maybe there'll be a job close to home."

"Everyone gets cabin fever this time of year," Wanda offered. "Seems like there's no end to the snow and cold. When are you gonna retire, Hank?"

"I intend to keep working as long as I got my health."

"There's a rumor that Boise-Cascade has something big in the works," she said.

Hank and Wanda suspected that the rumor had some connection to the trade unions' meeting with Boise-Cascade's management.

"It would be great if they gave us a new mill," She mused.. I could put this place up for sale at a decent price and retire to someplace where it stays warm all year. Lulu left for Florida just weeks after she sold it to me. She's never been back."

"Nothing's for certain," Jack cautioned. "All I can say is that Boise is preparing to make an announcement. Let's hope it's soon and that it'll mean jobs for the building trades."

Men in work clothes began filing in and Wanda grabbed her order pad and moved out from behind the counter. The new arrivals greeted her and nodded to Hank and Jack. Wanda circulated among the tables and booths, taking orders while she poured. Jack got up and stretched.

"Time to hit the road." He said. "Edith will have lunch waiting."

"When will you be back?" Hank asked.

"When Boise says it's ready to to make an announcement. If and when that will happen is anyone's guess. Until it happens, the rumor is only wishful thinking."

Jack left and Wanda returned to the counter with her coffee pot. "Can I get you something to take home for Mary?"

Hank shook his head, stood and reached for his wallet. She put a hand on his arm.

"It's on me. When you're workin' again, you can buy me a beer."

"When do you think Boise will make an announcement?" he asked.

"Soon," she assured him.

"What makes you think so?"

"Because you can't keep a secret very long in a town this small."

Chapter Two

On January 20, 1989, George Herbert Walker Bush was sworn in as the forty-first President of the United States. He was chosen to succeed Ronald Reagan despite a 1987 stock market crash and the recession that followed. "Read my lips," was the battle cry of the Bush campaign against a lackluster opponent. "No new taxes," was the promise that persuaded an electorate in no mood to share its good fortune as signs of an economic recovery began to appear.

In Bloomington, Minnesota, construction of the world's largest shopping mall was expected to create hundreds of jobs in the southern part of the state. Almost four hundred miles to the north, Boise-Cascade was preparing to announce a major expansion of its paper mill in International Falls. Together, the two projects would provide good-paying jobs for thousands in the construction industry.

"A new mill in International Falls will mean steady work for as many as two thousand trade union members over the next couple of years," Jack Ross told this ironworkers. "Once it's up and running, there could be as many as several hundred new paper-making and logging jobs. Take a look at what's been happening in Michigan."

In a tiny community in Michigan's Upper Peninsula, Champion International Corporation had been converting wood into pulp, the main component of paper. When Champion decided it could use its pulp to make high quality, coated paper, it began a substantial expansion of its mill in Quinnisec. Champion's general construction contractor was Rust Engineering and the workforce building Champion's new paper mill was mostly union. As Champion's mill project had done for Michigan's Upper Peninsula, an expansion of Boise-Cascade's mill in International Falls would provide good-paying jobs for the building trades in northern Minnesota.

In anticipation of an announcement by Boise-Cascade, Jack Ross began to placed telephone calls to local unions throughout the upper midwest.

"If Boise-Cascade undertakes a project in International Falls as large as the one that Champion has at Quinnisec, my small local union isn't going to be able to meet the demand for skilled ironworkers."

Jack knew he could not count on help from southern Minnesota where the labor pool was stretched thin by the mall being built in Bloomington. But construction was beginning to wind down at Quinnisec, and Jack was hoping that Michigan ironworkers soon would be looking for work elsewhere. Jack would also need a project agreement with Boise-Cascade's general construction contractor, and he would have to get subcontractors to sign. He hoped for an agreement that would set a high standard for ironworkers' wages and benefits in northern Minnesota. Although there was always tension during contract talks, he got along reasonably well with local employers with whom it rarely took a strike to get an agreement. Most negotiations ended with both sides feeling vindicated, and Jack was confident that getting an acceptable project agreement would not be difficult if a Boise-Cascade's plans were on a scale comparable to Champion's project at Quinnisec.

Jack was born in Hibbing, a small, northern Minnesota city on the Mesabi Iron Range, home of the world's largest open-pit taconite mine. Although he struggled to maintain a B average through high school, he excelled in hockey and football. After graduating, he went to work as a laborer for the mining company that employed both his father and two uncles. He tried to convince himself that he was honoring a family tradition, but he never rid himself of the feeling that he was being indentured. Yearning for a life less dreary, he fled to Duluth and enrolled in a union-sponsored apprenticeship program. Later, as a journeyman ironworker, he traveled to construction sites throughout the midwest and western states, working at heights that would turn most men's legs to jelly.

Nothing that Jack had experienced could compare to the thrill of walking a steel beam hundreds of feet above the ground and surveying a landscape that sprawled as far as the eye can see. When he finished a job, he knew that he had helped to build something that would last for decades and even longer. But the years take a toll on an ironworker's body and, by the time he was fifty-six, Jack was nursing a painfully degenerating spine. Forced to cease working as an ironworker, but unwilling to be completely separated from the trade, he became the elected business manager of his local union and found that trying to satisfy the expectations of its members could be as daunting as navigating the girders of a fledgling skyscraper.

The sedentary role of business manager added girth to Jack's waist, and his once thick brown hair receded and began to expose shiny glimpses of his scalp. He also lost some of the swagger that he exhibited as a member of a crew that built the Sears Tower in Chicago. The greatest risks that he took as chief spokesperson for his union was making decisions that impacted the livelihood of his members. To gain a concession when bargaining, he might have to give something in return. To please some he might be disappointing others.

"I try to get as much as I can by giving as little as possible," was how he put it. "Every *quid pro quo* poses a risk to my standing with the members whose votes keep me in office. Bargaining, like walking a beam, is a balancing act."

In 1989, after a winter of scarce opportunities for work, Jack's ironworkers were eager to be called off the bench. Union members who were fortunate enough to be sent to jobs in more friendly climates looked forward to returning to their homes in Minnesota. Others were nearing the end of their weekly unemployment checks. Some were behind in their house or car payments or had a vehicle that needed to be repaired or replaced. Homes need fresh paint or an extra room for child on the way. Daddy wanted power tools, momma fancied a new dress and baby needed a new pair of shoes. Everyone was hoping for an announcement from Boise-Cascade that would signal a season of steady work and paychecks. International Falls was ready to party.

When it finally came, Boise-Cascade's announcement of a five hundred and thirty-five million dollar expansion of its existing mill was delivered with the punch line of a cruel joke. The contract for the new construction had been awarded to BE&K, a southern company whose non-union workers would be arriving in vehicles with Texas, Louisiana, Arkansas, Mississippi and Alabama license plates. Only a small amount of work would be given to local subcontractors.

BE&K's bid for the Boise-Cascade contract was forty million dollars less than that of a rival bidder who would have employed Minnesota trade union members. Instead, local workers were going to be sitting on the sidelines. As an added insult, Boise-Cascade's expansion was being subsidized with sixteen million dollars in state tax credits. As taxpayers, Minnesota union members felt doubly betrayed.

Although BE&K paid wages only slightly less than prevailing union rates, BE&K workers did not receive all of the fringe benefits that union members enjoyed and BE&K's work rules were considered to be regressive. Union concerns went beyond disappointment over the loss of jobs. The hiring of BE&K was viewed as a direct assault upon the gains unions had made through collective bargaining.

"Scab labor puts pressure on our union contractors to ask to be released from promises they made at the bargaining table," Jack Ross explained. "Many of the benefits and working conditions that we enjoy were paid for with sacrifices made while walking a picket line. If BE&K's foray into Minnesota succeeds, the entire midwest will be a target for non-union contractors. Where will the Rat strike next? Wisconsin? Michigan? the Dakotas? Boise-Cascade's decision is unacceptable. We can't let BE&K have northern Minnesota."

Most of BE&K's workers were single men or men who left wives and families behind. BE&K housed them in furnished trailers installed in a large field behind a chain link fence at the edge of town. The workers in the "man camp" as it was called, were transported to and from the construction site by bus. BE&K paid a subsistence allowance to anyone willing to pay rent in town and commute to work. Those who came with families moved into neighborhoods where rental housing was available. The supply was limited, rents were inflated and landlords cheered.

BE&K subcontracted a small share of its work to local contractors, creating a dilemma for Jack Ross and other trade union leaders: Should they let their members work side by side with scabs or should they strike? And, if They strike, would the paper mill workers honor a building trades picket line?

The union representing Boise-Cascade's mill workers was wary. Several years earlier, when the workers at Boise-Cascade's paper mill in Rumford, Maine went on strike, they were replaced by non-union workers from other states. The strike was broken and several hundred union members, some with substantial Boise-Cascade seniority, lost their jobs.

"If the building trades strike here, in International Falls, and our mill workers refuse to cross the picket line, Boise-Cascade will replace them like it did in Rumford." Jack was warned.

"If we don't strike," he countered, "BE&K's scabs will be doing our work. That would set a precedent that we can't allow."

At a hastily called union meeting, Jack reminded his members that he never had been reluctant to strike in order to get a fair contract or to protest unsafe working conditions and yes, there were times when ironworkers went on strike against scabs doing their work.

"But BE&K is bringing a thousand scabs to this project, and it can bring a thousand more," he cautioned. "The numbers are against us."

"We'll picket the mill, too," someone shouted. "Its workers are union members. They'll refuse to cross our picket line and Boise will have to send BE&K packing."

"BE&K's scabs will cross a picket line," Jack continued, "and we're too few to stop them."

He told them about Rumford Maine " If the mill workers walk out in sympathy, the Rat will get the paper-making jobs."

There were groans followed by cheers when someone shouted, "I say we strike!"

"A strike will only halt the work of our union contractors," Jack went on: "If we refuse to work with scabs, we'll also be violating the 'no strike' clauses in our agreements with them. They'll sue and we will have squandered the good will that has benefited our relationships."

Members began to leave the meeting and, when someone called for a strike vote, Jack granted a motion to adjourn. Several days later, one hundred and fifty union tradesmen, Jack's ironworkers among them, walked off the Boise-Cascade expansion project. They stationed pickets at BE&K's construction gate. There were no pickets at the entrances to Boise-Cascade's paper mill.

Chapter Three

Union subcontractors whose striking employees refused to work with BE&K scabs were furious. They accused Jack and other union leaders of encouraging the strike with winks and nods. They demanded that the strikers be ordered to return to work and threatened to sue if the unions failed to persuade their members to end their walkout.

"This strike wasn't authorized by any union," Jack replied, " and we haven't given it our stamp of approval. We've told them to return to their jobs, but they are adamant. They refuse to work with scabs. Nothing we do or say is going to change their minds."

The strikers on the picket line wielded rudely lettered signs tacked to poles and stakes. They shouted insults and made obscene gestures as BE&K workers went through the gate. Vehicle doors and side panels were gouged and roofing nails were scattered on the street and in the driveway to the construction site. On weekends, tradesmen from the mill project at Quinnisec, Michigan, joined the picketing strikers. Their presence in International Falls gave rise to a belief among local contractors that Jack Ross and others were conspiring with out-of-state unions.

"That Michigan union members are coming here to picket should surprise no one,"Jack declared. "They have a stake in the fight against non-union competition and they have a right to protest. It's Boise-Cascade and BE&K that picked this fight. They knew that this is union territory. "

Each morning, a cadre of striking pickets assembled at the construction gate to begin their daily march. Although incidents on the picket line were few and relatively minor, acts of vandalism began occurring in neighborhoods where BE&K workers and families rented housing. Vehicles with southern license plates were spray-painted. Some had tires slashed. Homes where they were parked were pelted with eggs and rocks and windows were shattered. Incidents thought to be retaliatory began to occur in neighborhoods where BE&K had no presence. The vandalism took place under cover of darkness and few arrests were made.

"We're doing what we can,"said the Chief of Police, "but I can't have officers in every alley or on every street where out-of-state cars are parked during the night."

When a BE&K supervisor's car was torched and a homemade gasoline bomb destroyed an equipment shed in a Boise-Cascade supply yard, Boise hired a private security company. The arrival of armed, uniformed security guards sparked protests from the strikers.

"We're being harassed and threatened," they complained. "When we leave the picket line, the guards are following and photographing us. Something has to be done to make them stop."

The guards wore black, military-style uniforms, helmets and bullet-proof vests. Housewives and other shoppers complained that the presence of these baton-carrying strangers made them afraid to shop downtown. They demanded that the guards be confined to Boise-Cascade's property. Local people also began to look with suspicion and distrust upon anyone whose accent was southern. Some made little effort to hide their disdain for the newcomers. Merchants who did not appear to share that disdain fell out of favor and their customers began making fewer visits, choosing to do their shopping in nearby towns. The bonanza anticipated by the town's retailers never fully materialized.

Tension on the picket line increased as security guards returned insults and threats through the chain link fence that separated them from the strikers. The tension peaked on weekends when union members from Michigan joined the strike.

"If we don't stop the Rat in Minnesota, the next fight could be in Michigan. We intend to be here until the last scab is gone."

Despite the picketing, BE&K brought its workers to the construction site each morning and returned them to the man camp at the end of the day. There was nothing to suggest that they would be leaving and no indication that the mill expansion was being disrupted by the strike.

On a Friday in mid-August, after construction at Quinnisec shut down for the weekend, a group of trade union members preparing to carpool to International Falls for another weekend of picketing confronted the ironworkers' chief steward.

"We don't mind giving our weekends to the cause," they said, "but how long will this strike have to go on before we see some results?"

Buck Saari had no answer, and he got into his pickup truck and drove off. At a tavern in nearby Iron Mountain, he pulled two tables together with chairs for several workers who stayed behind. Tradesmen at

Quinnisec came from Upper Peninsula communities with names like Silver City, Copper Harbor, Iron River and Crystal Falls. Their ancestors were mostly from European countries, but they spoke English with an inflection similar to their Canadian neighbors. They wore flannel, denim and canvas. On Friday paydays, they cashed their checks, dined on pickled eggs, beef jerky, burgers, fries and beer and stayed late.

"How many went to Minnesota this weekend?" the bartender asked when he brought their pitchers of beer.

"I didn't count," Buck said, but I'd say it was a dozen, maybe more."

"International Falls must be at least eight hours going and eight coming back," the bartender observed. "That doesn't leave much time for picketing."

"What's your point?" Buck snapped.

The bartender retreated. When he returned, he asked, "Anyone for more pickled eggs? On the house."

Buck and the others knew that the strike wasn't having much of an impact. Perhaps that was why some were staying behind. He turned to an ironworker from L'Anse and asked,

"Why aren't you on your way to Minnesota? Haven't you been going most weeks from the start?"

"I promised my kid I'd take him to the Fair in Escanaba. It's something we do every year since me and his mom split up. I only get to see him on alternate weekends. I promised his mother, too."

"You won't be missed," said a pipe fitter from Rapid River. "The scabs are crossing the picket like we're invisible. Don't get me wrong. I'm all for getting rid of the 'em, but a picket line ain't gonna stop anyone as long as there's a paycheck waiting for them on the other side."

A millwright raised his glass as if to offer a toast: "Let's get 'em where they live. Let's trash the man camp."

He took a long swallow and set his glass down on the table, spilling his beer.

"We gotta kick some ass," someone added.

Buck shook his head. "Are you serious?"

"You bet we are," said the millwright. "We have to get union members from ll over the midwest to take a stand with us at International Falls. What's needed is a show of force."

"A show of force to do what?" Buck asked.

"To run the scabs off. Trash the place if that's what it takes. Send the scabs back to where they came from."

The bartender began refilling empty mugs. When he got to the millwright, he hesitated.

"It's okay," someone said. "I'm driving."

"If we organize a mass demonstration, there'll be expenses," Buck said. "It's a wildcat strike. It doesn't have any union support. We would have to rely on donations from individual members."

"We're workin' steady," the millwright declared. "We can take care of expenses without any help from our unions."

"It would help if we got one or two unions to put up some cash," Buck said. "I'll run it by my business manager. The rest of you should do the same."

The bartender set more beer on the table. The millwright grabbed a pitcher and poured. "This one's on me," he said, knocking his glass over.

During the night, firefighters in International Falls were dispatched to a home occupied by a BE&K construction worker and his family. Flames had climbed from trash and debris piled against an outside wall at the rear of the home. When fire trucks arrived, the flames had reached the second floor, filling it with smoke. By the time the fire was brought under control, the first floor was flooded and the second floor bedrooms at the rear of the home were severely smoke and water damaged. No one was injured, but the occupants, mom, dad and two, young children, had to be evacuated with the few belongings they were able to remove before smoke and heat made further salvage impossible.

The family was taken to a motel where they spent the rest of the night facing an uncertain future. Mom tearfully pleaded to return to Alabama. Caught between his wife's fear of further violence and his own fear of being destitute if he were to abandon his job, Dad was stricken with the realization that he might have to send his family away and remain behind, alone.

The next day, a fight broke out between rival groups of teenagers in Smokey Bear Park. Local youths clashed with youngsters from families of BE&K workers. The participants, both male and female, ranged in age from thirteen to sixteen. There were conflicting claims as to how the fight started, but police officers were told that it was preceded by name-calling, threats and challenges. Although no arrests were made, it was apparent that International Falls was being divided into rival camps. The hostility between them was becoming more intense as the start of a new school year drew near. Parents and teachers were uncertain as to how the situation would play out in classrooms and on school playgrounds.

Chapter Four

The Pardee family made the trip from Dothan, Alabama, to International Falls in Hiram Pardee's 1979 Chevrolet pickup truck. Their four-year-old daughter sat on her mother's lap. Their five-year old son was squeezed between mom and dad. They brought boxes and bags filled with clothing, towels, linens, blankets, pots, pans, dishes and utensils. They loaded these into the bed of the pickup together with a sewing machine and the few other items that they were able to fit beneath a canvas tarpaulin secured with tic-downs. The children slept during much of the northward journey. Hiram and his wife, Betsy, took turns driving and managed brief naps at highway rest areas.

    The Pardees came to northern Minnesota so that Hiram could work for BE&K as an equipment operator at the Boise-Cascade mill expansion, a project that they were told might last up to two years. Although Betsy had mixed feelings about leaving the familiar surroundings of her home town, Hiram's enthusiasm carried the day.

    "It's a job where I'll be able to earn more than I can ever hope to make in Dothan," Hiram stressed when he told Betsy of BE&K's offer,."It's gonna be an adventure, too, for you and the kids. Best of all, we'll have money in the bank by the time the job is done."

    Despite her initial misgivings, Betsy became almost as eager as her husband to escape the cramped quarters of their furnished, Dothan apartment and the oppressive heat of another Alabama summer. She began to look forward to the move as if they were about to venture to some exotic haven. Her husband could not have prepared her for the reception that awaited them in Minnesota.

    Hiram spent his childhood and youth in Henry County, Alabama. His family planted and harvested tomatoes, sweet peas and okra on a small farm a few miles west of Dothan. His father taught him to operate and maintain the farm's equipment which included a pickup truck, a flatbed grain truck, an ancient tractor and a backhoe. The family of three lived modestly on what they could extract from the land and the few farm animals and fowl that they raised. What they didn't consume, they sold at the farmers market in Dothan.

The Pardees were Baptists and attended church and church-sponsored events. Hiram's parents thought of themselves as conservative Democrats, but they abandoned Jimmy Carter and voted for Ronald Reagan twice, and George H. W. Bush once before switching their support to a former governor from Arkansas.

Hiram loved baseball and basketball, but school studies and farm work left him no time for organized sports. As a teenager, he displayed his athletic prowess under the schoolyard hoop and on the softball diamond during recess and summer vacations.

After struggling through high school with average grades, Hiram settled for a minimum-wage job in an automotive repair shop where he remained until BE&K hired him and trained him to operate and maintain several pieces of heavy equipment, including a front end loader and grader. The job kept him on the move from one construction site to another throughout much of the south. The pay was a substantial improvement over what he had been earning in the repair shop.

During several periods of temporary layoff, Hiram found time to meet, fall in love with and briefly court Elizabeth Barnwell, a petite southern beauty and former high school classmate. They married despite the protestations of Betsy's mother who wanted a more suitable groom for her only child. Years earlier, after making a small fortune speculating in pork belly futures, Betsy's father abandoned his wife and infant daughter. Before he died, he sent them money from time to time, not enough for the luxuries that Betsy's mother coveted, but enough to allow them to live comfortably. Hiram Pardee was not going to fill the void.

"It would have been just as easy to fall in love with a man of means," Betsy's mother scolded on more than one occasion after Betsy and Hiram married.

Betsy had two miscarriages before giving birth to a son, Rodney. When Grace came along a year later, Betsy began to yearn for a time when she and Hiram could settle into a more stable and comfortable lifestyle, one that Hiram's transient work for BE&K did not allow. When Hiram traveled with his construction crew, Betsy spent much of her time with her mother, listening to the old woman complain about her daughter's choice of a husband. But Betsy was resolute in defense of Hiram.

"My husband is faithful and hard-working," she argued whenever she could get a word in. "He adores me and the children, which is something no amount of money can buy. We are a couple."

"Humf," was her mother's reply. "You'll sing a different tune when you're my age, but by then it will be too late."

Betsy learned to turn a deaf ear to her mother's complaints and the opportunity to move to International Falls was somewhat of a dream come true. Hiram would have a lengthy period of steady work, Betsy would be free of her mother's carping and there would be money with which to plan a future. The somber greeting given to the Pardee family in the unfamiliar place to which they migrated diminished Betsy's enthusiasm. What little remained was extinguished by the fire that left the Pardees homeless and added fear to their isolation.

Buck Saari placed a telephone call to his local union business manager in Marquette and asked for money to help pay for a bus to transport ironworkers and others from Quinnisec to International Falls.

"We have to stop the Rat in International Falls. If scabs are allowed to steal our work in Minnesota, Michigan could be next. Picketing is getting us nowhere. It's time to take a more aggressive stand."

"If the union pays for a bus to to take members International Falls, what are they going to do other than picket when they get there?"

"We're planning a rally. We'll be asking hundreds to participate in a mass demonstration of support for the strike. I need money for the bus and driver for those who will be going from Quinnisec."

"What about the other trade unions? Will they be contributing?"

"We'll be asking them to pitch in."

"You mean they're not on board yet."

"We're just getting started."

"What are you going to need besides money?"

"Publicity. Something that can be handed out at Quinnisec and other jobs. Some kind of announcement. A leaflet."

In order to give himself time to persuade ironworkers and other trade union members to participate, Buck decided to hold the rally on September 9, the Saturday after Labor Day. Many of the scabs would not be working on a Saturday. He would have his union members, hundreds of them, assemble at the man camp's chain link fence. Maybe they would take the rally into the man camp.

In a three-star motel on the outskirts of International Falls, Hiram sat on a vinyl- covered swivel chair in front of a small writing desk. His four-year-old daughter, Grace, was sitting with Betsy on one of the two beds that filled most of the room. The girl sniffled and dabbed her eyes with a tissue that her mother handed her. Rodney, the five year old, sat next to his sister. His blank expression revealed nothing of what that he was feeling as he listened to the adults.

"I can't help it" Betsy said." I'm afraid for the children and I want to take them home. Can't you see that we ain't wanted here? We haven't been since the day we got here. And. now this…this…fire. This ain't a place for our children to be raised. Let's go home. Please."

Grace was nestled against her mother. Betsy put an arm around her and looked down at the child's blond head and small, frail shoulders. The boy, hearing his mother's words, turned to look at his father who was staring at the floor.

Hiram was a tall, lanky southerner with a weathered face, high cheek bones and close-cropped, reddish hair. His shoulders sloped and his gangly arms and long legs made him look like someone who would feel at home behind a plow. His wife, Elizabeth, whom he called "Betsy," was much shorter, with wide hips, a thick waist and modest breasts. Her small mouth and nose and smooth complexion hinted that she might have been pretty as a child, but as she pleaded with Hiram, her face was swollen and her eyes were puffy and red, even though they were no longer tearful.

"Hasn't this fire been enough?" she asked. "What more is it gonna take to convince you?"

Hiram looked up and turned to face her, leaning forward with his elbows on his knees. His voice was little more than a whisper.

"This is the best job I ever had. It's better'n anything I'll be able to find if I go back to Alabama. It's a chance for you and me and the kids to have a better life. If I leave now, B E&K will never take me back." He paused and took a deep breath. "So, tell me what you want me to do. Do you want me to quit and put us on welfare?"

Betsy stared at her husband and shook her head. Not wanting to repeat words she had already spoken and unable to think of anything to add, she waited for Hiram to continue.

"If we save enough money, I can get my own engine repair shop when I'm done with this job. We'd move back to Dothan and I wouldn't have to travel. We could have a real home. But for now, I don't see how I can do any better than what I'm doin' here, in Minnesota."

"I know how you feel," she sobbed, "and I ain't sayin' your job's not important, but…"

"We can find us another place to live," he said, "in a better neighborhood. But I need this job and I need you and the kids to be with me. We're a family."

Betsy fought off tears and got her second wind.

"You don't know what it's like for me and the kids. You go off to work and maybe there's some whooping and hollering at the gate, but you go in and come out with the others that you work with. You got nothin' to be scared of. I can't even take the children to the grocery store without gettin' mean looks from the local women and nasty comments behind my back. They think I don't hear them, but I do and it scares me."

Her eyes began to tear and she looked over at the boy.

"And what about Rodney?" she asked. "He'll be starting school in a few weeks. What about him?"

At the sound of his name, the boy turned to look at his mother. Their eyes met briefly before he turned away.

"If we stay here," she continued, "he'll have be in school with the same bullies that tease him and call him names when he goes out to play. 'Rat,' they call him, and 'scab,' and sometimes with the older ones it's even worse."

She held a tissue to her nose and blew.

"And now the place that was our home since we been here is burnt to the ground and we're stuck in a motel for who knows how long. It ain't right, 'specially for the children. We have to get away from here and go home. Please."

Her tears were flowing, and now Grace was sobbing, too. But Rodney, listening, hands folded on his lap, betrayed no emotion.

Chief David Patterson, of the International Falls Police department met with Jack Ross whose striking union members were under suspicion for reasons that Patterson thought should be obvious to everyone in International Falls.

"If you think the members of my union are responsible for the vandalism you are seriously mistaken, " Jack protested. "There's not one among them who would do ny of these things. They certainly wouldn't commit arson. We are not the ones you should be questioning."

Jack had to admit, if only to himself, that some of the vandalism was probably strike-related, but he was also prepared to argue that there was provocation.

"Boise-Cascade must have known there'd be a reaction if it brought the Rat to a union town. If Boise had hired a union contractor, we wouldn't be having this conversation. Of course my members are upset. Why shouldn't they be? Truth is the whole town's upset, and with good reason."

"I'm not asking you to point a finger at anyone," the Chief said. "I'm asking you to do what you can to discourage your people from engaging in behavior that will land them in jail. Tell them to confine their protest to the picket line and spare me from the unpleasantness of arrests and prosecutions. That's what will happen to anyone caught breaking the law."

Chapter Five

Roger Beaudre hoped that his absence from the picket line would not be noticed or would be forgotten by the following weekend. He kept his promise and took his son to the Upper Peninsula Fair, an event that lingers in a youngster's memory from one year to the next. Nick Beaudre, who was a few months shy of his fourteenth birthday, was almost as tall as his five foot, eight inch, thirty-six-year-old father. Tempered by the physical demands of his labor as an ironworker, Roger was lean and agile. Nick was developing a similar physique, one that already served him well on the hockey rink where he performed almost as skillfully as his father once had.

During the winter months, when work in construction is slack, the senior Beaudre volunteered as an assistant coach in a hockey program for skaters under the age of fifteen. Roger, who was fiercely competitive, knew that Nick hungered for his father's approval and would strive to excel. He also believed that it was never too early to inspire a youngster. On their way to Escanaba, father and son shared their expectations for the winter hockey season.

"The forecast is for an early winter with frigid temperatures and lots of snow," Roger said. "The coaches have been telling me that there will be a lot of talent in the league this year. You better be ready for some stiff competition."

In mid-August, when the Upper Peninsula's summer tourist season reaches its peak, highway traffic is slowed by motor homes and vehicles towing campers and watercraft. It wasn't until they turned onto southbound highway 141 that Roger was able to increase speed from Covington to Crystal Falls. He slowed when he got into eastbound traffic on U.S. 2, across northern Wisconsin and back into Michigan in Iron Mountain, an hour from their destination.

"Are we almost there?" Nick asked. "I'm hungry."

"Me too. There'll be plenty to eat when we get to the Fair. I'm looking forward to the Croatian chicken. What about you?"

Nick was thinking of corn dogs, elephant ears and root beer.

Roger grew up in the small community of L'Anse, on the southeast shore of Keweenaw Bay. His youthful ambition to play professional hockey was thwarted when he was permanently banned from his college team after he attacked and seriously injured an opposing team member. Convicted of aggravated assault, he was sentenced to an extended period of supervised probation that included a program of anger management.

"Hockey is a rough sport," was Roger's explanation when Nick asked about his father's storied clash with the law "It's best to keep your stick on the ice and your eye on the puck."

"Is that the only time you've been in trouble with the law?" Nick asked

"Yeah. That was my first and last." Roger said.

In keeping with his desire to be a role model, he made no mention of the time he knocked a classmate to the ground and was attempting to kick him as he was pulled away during a fist fight at a fraternity party. The fallen classmate declined to press charges, and the young lady for whose attention the two were contesting never spoke to Roger again.

When a future as a hockey star was no longer on his horizon, Roger dropped out of college and returned to L'Anse where he worked for a short while in a mill that manufactured ceiling tiles. When he grew tired of the job, he moved to Marquette and enrolled in an ironworkers apprentice program. He became a journeyman, returned to L'Anse and married.

The ironworker trade often kept Roger away from home for weeks and occasionally for months at a time. His transient lifestyle failed to satisfy his young bride's expectations for the marriage, but they remained together long enough for her to have Roger's child. After Nick was born, she decided to end the marriage before more children came along. Despite the divorce, the relationship remained amicable and Roger was determined to be a good father to his son. His weekend parenting was disrupted when he was recruited by Buck Saari to picket at International Falls with other Quinnsec workers.

"We need to draw a line in International Falls," Buck told him. "A display of solidarity with our striking, union brothers in Minnesota will discourage non-union competition from trying to get a foothold in Michigan."

BE&K workers, who didn't look much different than the men who were picketing, were impervious to cries of "stop the Rat,"and"scabs go home." Obscenities and empty threats seemed pointless. Only a few of the guards were responding in kind. That the strike was keeping Roger from his son on weekends added to Roger's angst.

It was a few minutes past noon when the two drove into the fairground parking lot. The temperature had climbed to eighty degrees and parking spaces were filling rapidly. At the gated entrance to the fairground, Roger purchased tickets while Nick went on ahead. Roger had to run to catch up and keep from losing Nick in the crowd. They slow-walked the livestock and poultry barns, visited the craft and junior art exhibits, viewed the produce displays and inspected an array of new farm machinery. Afterward, they sat in the grandstand, eating corn dogs. Roger drank lemonade and Nick had his root beer as they watched a horse-drawn plow pulling exhibition.

"When this is over, can we go back to the barns?" Nick asked.

The request took Roger by surprise and he wondered what had caught the boy's attention. When they joined a crowd waiting to witness the birth of a calf, the mystery was solved.

"Awesome," Nick exclaimed when it as over.

On the midway, Roger purchased tickets for carnival rides and watched Nick being strapped into a miniature spaceship. It was launched skyward, spinning and tumbling before reaching a peak and plummeting almost to the ground. When it rocketed skyward again in a series of ascents and descents, Roger, began to feel queasy. When it was over, Nick, breathless, came rushing toward him.

"C'mon Dad," he shouted, pointing. "The next one's called 'Zero Gravity."

It was a huge cylinder rising, spinning and pinning those inside to its inner wall. Roger took another pass, but agreed to ride with Nick on the Ferris Wheel.

"I'm okay with heights," he explained, "but spinning, not so much."

The evening's entertainment was a popular country-western singer, but shortly before the show was to begin, father and son decided that they had enough. After a brief search of the parking lot, they found their pickup truck. During the ride home, Roger thought about the rally Buck was planning. Was it to be mass picketing? What did Buck hope to accomplish with more pickets at the gate, and if they rallied at the man camp, how would the scabs react? Nick fell sleep with his head resting against his father's shoulder, and Roger felt better about not having spent the weekend in International Falls.

Theodore Grissom, owner of Ted's Northern Tours, assured Buck that he could provide a bus that would accommodate as many as fifty passengers.

"Bus and driver will cost fifteen hundred, paid in cash before we leave. No refunds. I can be waiting for you and be ready to board in Iron Mountain and can bring you back the next day."

"What's included?" Buck asked.

"I'm not in the catering business," Grissom replied. "Bring your own food and liquid refreshments."

"My mind's made up," Betsy told Hiram. "It seems the fire wasn't enough to convince you it ain't safe here, but I'm scared and so are Rodney and Grace. The children shouldn't have to be afraid. Stay if you must. We're goin' home."

It was decided that Hiram would drive them to Duluth and put them on the first of several Greyhound coaches that would take them to Montgomery, Alabama. Betsy's mom would meet them there and bring them the rest of the way to Dothan. Hiram gave Betsy money for meals along the way and promised to send more each payday. She needed to be frugal, but she purchased a few coloring books and crayons and packed them with as much clothing rescued from the fire as her battered suitcase would hold. She would have to manage her one piece of luggage along with the children.

"If we leave International Falls early in the morning, we can get to Duluth with time to spare," Hiram told her. "You'll be able to sleep once you're on the bus."

"Mother will put us up in Dothan. We'll only stay with her until I find a place we can afford. Maybe the apartment we had before we left is still available. I'll start there. And don't worry about the children," she added. "Mother adores them."

He was thinking that his mother-in-law would probably try to turn Betsy and the children against him, but he felt he had to remain in Minnesota as long as BE&K had work for him. Betsy would have to manage without him. She would have the children to comfort her until the separation was over.

"I'll stay in the man camp until the job is done. That's' the least expensive way I can get by and be able to send money."

If he could not send her enough, Betsy would have to ask her mother to help. That was a prospect he didn't want to think about. He promised to pack and ship more of her belongings. She mentioned clothing and shoes, a box of costume jewelry, a few framed photographs and some other things that she was leaving behind. He would need boxes. Not many. Most of what they owned had been ruined in the fire. He wondered how he would wrap and seal the boxes, and what it would cost to ship them. His next payday was two weeks away. The boxes would have to wait.

They were silent during the last half hour of the drive to Duluth. The children were silent, too. In Duluth, Hiram dropped them at the door to the bus terminal and went looking for a place to park. When he returned, he found them snacking on potato chips and sharing a large soft drink near a bank of vending machines.

"This'll have to hold us 'til we get to Minneapolis," Betsy said, offering him some chips. "We can get sandwiches to share while we're waiting for the next bus. Are you sure you won't change your mind and come with us?"

He tried to imagine the welcome he'd receive from her mother. "I got a job to do here. I need it so there can be money for you and the children. Soon as it's finished, I'll come home."

While the Pardees waited for the bus that would take Betsy and the children on the first leg of their southbound journey, a northbound coach from Minneapolis arrived at the terminal and discharged its passengers. Among them was a tall, broad-shouldered man in his mid-thirties. He was wearing baggy camouflage pants and a black turtleneck sweater. A sweatband circled his shaved head, and a canvass duffle bag hung at his side from a strap slung over his shoulder. His stride was purposeful, and he was barely conscious of the weight of the bag as he moved through the crowded terminal. He brushed past the Pardees without noticing them.

Chapter Six

Tyrone Gates stepped out of the bus terminal and onto West Michigan Street to wait for the company limo that was to take him to International Falls. He listened to the greetings and goodbyes of people entering and leaving the terminal. Their banal chatter and midwestern accents amused him.

Tyrone grew up in Murfreesboro, Tennessee, as the only child of a submissive mother who took in other people's laundry and ironing for meager pay, and a father who owned and managed a saloon in a working class neighborhood. The senior Gates divided his time between pouring shots for patrons sitting at the bar and downing shots behind it. When sober, he was an attentive husband and affectionate father. When drunk, he was a self-hating brute who used his fists to vent his rage upon his wife and son.

During his teen years, Tyrone was figuratively and literally a big man on his high school campus, earning letters in football and wrestling. His physical stature and athletic accomplishments also earned him the flirtatious attention of the school's cheerleaders, including one who rewarded his advances with intimate favors. During his senior year, a hushed pregnancy and abortion spared him from a scandal that would have cost him the respect of his teammates and coaches.

Tyrone's high school celebrity faded rapidly after he graduated. The only work that he was able to find, stocking shelves at a local supermarket, had neither the glamour of the football field nor the exhilaration of a wrestling match. He missed the envy of his former high school buddies and the adoration of his female entourage. When his father attempted to thrash Tyrone with a belt during an argument, the six foot, three, one hundred and ninety-pound, nineteen-year-old struck back, knocking the elder Gates down with a single, roundhouse blow that the old man was too slowed by age and booze to avoid. Tyrone stormed out of the house, leaving his tearful mother kneeling beside her inebriated husband who was lying unconscious on the living room floor.

Hoping to regain some of the prestige and self-esteem that he enjoyed in high school, Tyrone replaced his stock clerk's apron with the uniform of a United States Marine. Determined to excel, he trained rigorously and became proficient in several martial arts. He was rewarded with an assignment as a guard in a military correctional facility. During the rest of his service to his country, he processed prisoners for confinement and release, supervised their daily activities, performed routine inspections and reported infractions of prison regulations to higher authorities. To his lasting disappointment he never saw combat, having served long after the Viet Nam war ended. When honorably discharged, he had the ambivalent self-esteem of a highly skilled warrior who had never been tested on the battlefield.

With his military career behind him, Tyrone settled in Memphis where he was able to find work as a warehouse laborer during the day and as a strip club bouncer at night. In the warehouse, moving crates with a forklift left him without a sense of achievement. As a bouncer, he earned a reputation for using excessive force and once was charged with criminal assault after ejecting an unruly patron. The case had to be dismissed when his alleged victim failed to appear for trial. Although Tyrone felt that his skill as a military combatant was being squandered on drunks and fools, his enthusiasm for physical contact captured the attention of a strip club patron who was a former Navy Seal employed by a private security company .

"The Alderton Security and Protection Corporation can always use another good man," Tyrone's new and eager sponsor declared. "If you will submit an application, I will introduce and recommend you to my boss."

No mention was made of the recruitment fee to be paid to the sponsor if Tyrone's application were accepted. After passing a pre-employment physical examination, Tyrone was hired and given a few short term, late night assignments in factory and warehouse settings. The work was uninspiring and when an assignment of greater duration and the possibility of physical conflict was offered, Tyrone accepted. Maintaining order among striking and potentially unruly construction workers seemed infinitely more challenging than clubbing rats in a deserted warehouse at night.

Tyrone traveled by bus to Duluth where he had a short wait in front of the bus terminal before climbing into the limo that was to deliver him to his new assignment in International Falls. While he waited for his ride, Betsy and the Pardee children boarded the bus that would take them to Minneapolis, the first stop on their way to Dothan. Rodney scrambled onto a window seat. His sister pouted when she was lifted into place next to her brother. Betsy sat across from them for only a few minutes before taking the sulking girl onto her lap. By the time his pickup truck was ten minutes out of Duluth, Hiram was regretting that he had not boarded the bus with his family.

Tyrone was dropped off at a motel in International Falls where he was greeted by a supervisor and introduced to several off-duty guards with whom he would be working. He was told that he would be fitted for an Alderton Security and Protection Corporation uniform, helmet and body armor. A baton, pepper spray, five-cell flashlight and other gear would be assigned to him at the guard shack where work schedules were posted.

"Union members, who we also refer to as 'thugs,' are picketing illegally," the supervisor explained. "They are threatening to assault anyone crossing their picket line and they are willing to destroy private property in order to intimidate Boise-Cascade and BE&K employees. Although we are here to discourage these thugs, you should exercise restraint when responding to insults or threats from the picket line, and use caution during off-duty encounters. Local law enforcement officers are strike sympathizers and they are looking for excuses to harass us."

Tyrone was asked by his new co-workers to join them for drinks at a tavern on Highway 53, several miles south of the motel. They left in an unmarked Buick, one of several leased to their employer.

The Beaver Dam Bar and Grill once was a place where local patrons enjoyed fish fries on Friday nights and prime rib dinners on Saturday. During the week, it was a popular place for a beer or cocktail after work. In summer, it was where tourists could find temporary escape from crowded campgrounds. The Beaver Dam's atmosphere changed when BE&K's construction crews arrived. Men with southern accents and fat paychecks filled the place every night of the week. They spent liberally, tipped generously and kept the waitstaff hustling and the cash registers ringing. Extra help had to be brought in from neighboring counties and from cities as far away as Duluth and Minneapolis. It was rumored that some of the waitresses were earning extra pay in a back room after hours.

Sitting at a table with his new companions, Tyrone eyed the waitress that took their drink order. She wore a miniskirt and a sleeveless blouse. When she served drinks, she leaned forward and revealed some cleavage. A few years earlier, she could have been one of Tyrone's high school cheerleaders She was attractive enough to make Tyrone feel a bit of nostalgia for his letter-sweater days. He gave her a flirtatious wink with his food order.

"T-bone medium rare, side salad and baked potato," she repeated.

"And you for dessert," he added.

She acted as if she didn't hear, and turned to the others at the table. It was steaks all around and more drinks. Tyrone watched her hips sway as she walked toward the kitchen. He thought that she was someone he should get to know. He hadn't noticed if she was wearing a ring, but decided that it didn't matter and wondered if others at the table were having similar thoughts.

By the time they finished eating, the crowd had thinned and there were empty tables. The noise had diminished, too, even though a fan of Merle Haggard was still feeding the jukebox. At the bar a fat patron was groping the mini-skirted waitress. She wasn't pleased. When he slipped a hand under her skirt, she let out a squeal and tried to pull away, but he had his other arm around her waist, holding her against him. The bartender's back was turned and no one seemed to notice except Tyrone who felt a sudden rush of adrenaline like when he worked the strip club in Memphis and had to deal with unruly drunks.

He was on his feet and moving to the bar, where he threw an arm around the fat guy's neck, jerking him backwards and off his stool. The waitress shrieked and pulled away. The bartender turned and stared. Tyrone's dinner party was up, grabbing at him and telling him to let go. He released his grip and stepped back, allowing his victim to stumble toward the door and out to the parking lot beyond.

"Save that stuff for the job," one of Tyrone's companions counseled. "You ain't gettin' paid to rescue barmaids."

"Maybe she'll give him a reward," another quipped.

"You want another drink?" she asked, having regained her composure. "On the house," she added.

"Them, too?" Tyrone asked, hooking a thumb toward the others.

She looked at the bartender and he gave her a nod.

"Sure," she said. "But don't get ideas. The drinks are the only reward you're gonna get."

Chapter Seven

By the time Hiram reached International Falls after putting Betsy and the children on the bus in Duluth, the sun was setting and he was thirsting for a cold drink. Bringing the family north was a mistake. He would move into the man camp and be with other men until the work was done. Before he checked in, he wanted to be alone with his thoughts and a cold beer. He heard stories about the good time that could be had at a tavern called the Beaver Dam, but he doubted that it was a place where he should stop, even though his Alabama draw would likely go unnoticed. He drove aimlessly through unfamiliar neighborhoods until he found himself on a street with darkened storefronts on one side and clapboard houses on the other. The street seemed deserted and was dark except for a street lamp in the middle of the block and a blinking neon sign at the end of the row of storefronts. Seeing no parked vehicles, he pulled to the curb beyond the street lamp, shut off the engine and turned off the lights of his pickup truck. He sat there for several minutes before getting out and walking the remaining half block to Benny's Saloon. He failed to notice the sign above the door before he pulled it open and stepped inside.

In the dimly lighted interior, tables and chairs were empty except for four men who appeared to be playing cards at one of the tables. There was a pool table in the middle of the room and a jukebox and some empty booths against a far wall. A barmaid was sitting alone on a stool at the end of the bar. She turned and looked at Hiram, but remained seated. Hiram thought the men at the table might be looking at him, too, and he avoided eye contact as he stepped up to the bar. The barmaid got off her stool and came around to face him from behind the bar.

"What'll you have?" she asked in a voice that seemed coarse but not unfriendly.

Most of her customers lived in the neighborhood. Hiram was not one of them. She had not seen him before, but did not ask if he had seen the sign above the door. She did not think that the old men at the table were likely to cause any trouble.

"Beer," Hiram said, lowering his eyes while digging in his jeans for the couple of dollars he had held back when he put his family on the bus.

"Bottle, can or draft?" she asked.

"Don't matter."

When he looked up, she was staring at him.

"Whatever you got on tap," he said.

She rattled off several names that he hadn't heard before, except one.

"Bud Light," he said, settling for what he favored back home in Alabama. "Did you say you got it on tap?"

She shrugged and moved a few feet away to fill a tall glass before setting it in front of him.

"You wanna start a tab?"

He shook his head and laid a dollar on the bar.

"One-fifty," she said.

He glanced at the corner table again, before reaching for another dollar bill and putting it on the bar.

"Keep the change."

He regretted his words as soon as they were out of his mouth. He didn't know how much money he had in his pocket. He hadn't counted what was left after he paid for the bus tickets.

The barmaid turned to the cash register on the back bar. She was taller than Betsy and younger by a couple of years. Her shoulders were narrow, her waist was slim and her slacks hugged a narrow behind. In bed, she would not be as ample a partner as Betsy. With his thoughts came a feeling of emptiness. It would be months before he would hold Betsy close again. He tried to picture himself with his arms around the barmaid, cupping her breasts. Unable to sustain the image, he lifted his glass and looked away.

A pair of hands slapped down on the bar and someone hoisted himself onto the stool next to Hiram. A voice broke the quiet of the room and the men at the table looked up from their card game. Seeing that it was one of Benny's regulars, they looked away.

"How's it goin', Deb? Not much action tonight, hey? Bring me some change for the juke box. I'll see if I can liven things up a bit."

He laid a few dollar bills and some change on the bar, grinning as if he expected an enthusiastic response from Debbie.

"How come you're not at the game?" she asked. "That's where the action is tonight. It's the season's opener."

She grabbed a bottle from the back bar, poured a shot of Jameson and set it in front of him. Then she filled a mug with beer and set it next to the shot.

"Same reason they ain't at the game," he said, hooking a thumb toward the men at the table. "We ain't fans of high school football."

The men at the table looked to be in their seventies or early eighties. Engrossed in their card game, they paid no attention to the pair at the bar.

"How 'bout you?" he asked, turning to Hiram. "Are you a football fan?"

Hiram shook his head.

"You got kids in high school?"

"Nope."

"Me either. Fact is, I got no kids."

Hiram studied his half-empty glass of beer. There was a bit of foam around the edge and a few bubbles were still rising from the bottom.

"I might not even have a wife much longer," the man continued. "She's pissed off 'cuz I ain't workin'. Says she's gonna go home to her mama. What do you think about that?"

Hiram didn't know what to think about that. He lifted his glass and took a long, slow swallow before setting the glass down and wiping his mouth with the back of his hand. Debbie, a few feet away, watched from behind the bar.

"I guess you don't have to think about it one way or the other," the man said. "It's my problem and you're probably thinking it ain't your business. Right?"

"If you say so," Hiram muttered. He was thinking it was time to finish his beer and leave.

"I s'pose you're happily married."

"Uh, huh."

"You look kinda' familiar. Do I know you?"

"Uh, uh."

"You sure?"

"Yep."

"You live around here?"

"Nope."

"I didn't think so. You ain't one of them scabs are you? I mean, well, you know what I mean."

Hiram sighed.

"Yeah. I'm workin construction at the paper mill, but I ain't lookin' to start trouble. I'll just finish my beer and be on my way."

He finished his beer with a couple of gulps and slid off of the bar stool. Debbie moved to the end of the bar, but her eyes remained on the two men.

"No offense," said the one still sitting and smiling as he turned on his barstool to face Hiram who was standing. "I was just asking 'cuz we don't usually see your kind in this part of town. Know what I'm sayin'?"

Hiram nodded, uncertain whether the man's smile was sincere.

"I been on the picket line most days since the strike began," the man said. "We see you people going across and through the gate day after day. It's hard not knowing how long it will go on. But hey, your glass is empty. Let me buy you one."

He wasn't very big, almost a head shorter than Hiram, but he looked lean and hard like a construction worker. Hiram thought he'd be able to take him on if he had to. There was also a football game, but another beer was tempting and the offer seemed genuine. He nodded to Debbie and she brought fresh glasses.

"What time is that football game supposed to end?" Hiram asked

"In another half hour or so I would imagine," She began wiping the bar while keeping an eye on the two men

Hiram lifted his glass in a salute and set it down.

"Name's Hiram. Thanks for the beer."

"No problem. I'm Jerome. Some call me Jerry, but mostly it's Jerome."

They shook hands. Debbie put her bar rag down and poured another shot for Jerome.

"You're from down south, ain't you?" Jerome asked, "like maybe Kentucky or Tennessee.

"Alabama. Dothan to be exact."

"I'm born and raised right here in the Falls," Jerome replied. "Been here all my life except when I have to go out'a town for work. But now there ain't any work and my wife's pissed off. Is that my fault? It's you southerners that took our jobs. Did you know that?"

"Don't know nothin' about that. Boss said he's got work in Minnesota, so we're workin' in Minnesota. That's about all I know."

"I been on the picket line, like I already said. Maybe that's where I seen you before. You ever see me there?"

"Might have. Can't help but see the picket line, but I'm only here to do a job. I don't figure the picket line is any of my business."

"Of course it's your business. Don't you get it? They was supposed to be union jobs. You took 'em from us. That's why we call you 'scabs. We're trying to run you off so we can have the work."

"Don't know nothin' bout that either. The picket line is for the bosses and the ones that are higher up."

"Damn the bosses and the higher-ups, man. You got a job to go to and I don't. Summer's almost done, and my wife says she's gonna leave me. Why is that my fault?"

He leaned closer to Hiram.

"If a bunch of guys from Minnesota went down to Alabama and took your jobs, would that be okay? I mean, would it? Think about that."

Hiram slid off of his bar stool again.

"I guess I'll be leaving but thanks again for the beer."

"What's the hurry? It's early yet. "

Jerome waved at Debbie and pointed to Hiram's half-empty glass. "One more."

Hiram shook his head . "It's been a long day and I got to be up early."

Jerome drained his beer with a gulp and set his glass down.

"Right. Early. You don't wanna be late for work, but hey," Jerome continued, "if you wanna have a beer with me again some time, it's okay. But listen. If you see me on the picket line, you don't know me. Know what I mean?"

Hiram nodded, turned to Debbie and nodded again. She smiled back at him as he started for the door.

Outside, the air was cool and fresh. Cars were pulling to the curb on both sides of the street. A few people were approaching on foot. A woman gave Hiram a curious look as they passed one another. The man whose arm she was holding didn't seem to notice. Hiram got into his pickup and started the engine. He wondered if he would recognize Jerome or if Jerome would remember him if they saw each other at the construction gate. As he pulled away from the curb, he glanced at the tavern and noticed the sign above the entrance.

"Union Only."

Chapter Eight

Winters in the Upper Peninsula are long and harsh, especially in the northernmost regions where snow can begin to fall as early as September and can continue into April and even the early days of May. The prevailing north wind coming across Lake Superior from Canada brings frigid snow and temperatures that sometime remain below freezing for weeks. As the wind continues southward, snow diminishes and temperatures moderate making Escanaba, a city of about twelve thousand inhabitants, the "banana belt"of the Upper Peninsula. In summer, southerly winds crossing Lake Michigan bring cool temperatures to the lakes north shore. As the wind continues northward over land, it moderates, warming Marquette on the southern shore of Lake Superior. In winter outdoor enthusiasts take to the the peninsula's ski hills and snowmobile trails. In summer, they enjoy forested campgrounds and pristine lakes and streams.

On a sunny afternoon in August, Ernie Hunter, known to some as Ernie the Attorney, took a telephone call in his office in Escanaba. When the conversation ended, he put the phone down, sighed, picked it up again and dialed. Ernie hated evening meetings, but Frank LeClaire, the business manger of a Michigan ironworkers local union, had a note of urgency in his voice and Ernie agreed to meet with him in Marquette.

"You'll have to have dinner without me," he told his wife, "and don't wait up. I might be home late."

"You know I'll worry if you're going to be driving in the dark," she said.

"I've done it dozens of times," he reminded her, "The moon and stars will be shining and I won't even need my headlights."

"Not funny," she said, "but what about your dinner? I can make something for myself, but where are you going to eat?"

"Frank and I will grab a bite while I'm in Marquette."

"Be sure to do that and let me know if you decide to stay over. Maybe I should call ahead and get you a motel room. I don't want you falling asleep at the wheel."

"Don't be silly. It's hardly more than an hour's drive. I'll call you if it looks like I won't be home by midnight."

After he hung up, he thought about her offer to get a room He picked the phone up again, but didn't dial. He did not care to sleep alone.

Ernie turned off of U.S. 2 at Gladstone. Northbound on M35, he passed through the villages of Perkins and Rock with their frame homes, rustic taverns and antiquated churches. From Lathrop to McFarland there were a few dilapidated house trailers and deserted hunting camps tucked into clearings in the woods. At Little Lake, several pickup trucks were parked in front of Brown's Tavern, and a few miles further, he made a right turn at a corner convenience store and gas station whose pumps were busy. He continued on County Road 553, past K.I. Sawyer Air Force base, through Sands Township and across County Road 480. When a sharp curve and a steep descent brought him to the bottom of several snowless ski slopes where empty lift chais dangled motionless above a carpet of summer green. If it had been winter, Rachel would have insisted on coming with him and they would have brought their skis.

"I'm surprised that you aren't leading the charge," Frank LeClaire told Jack Ross. "I would have expected you to be picketing with your members, but I heard that you refused to take a strike vote. Is that true?"

"It's easy to second guess, especially if you don't have to live with the consequences," Jack replied. "You have no serious non-union competition in the Upper Peninsula. "

"Not yet. But if BE&K brings its scabs to Michigan, there will be hell to pay, for sure."

"We both understand why my guys are striking," Jack said."But we also know that they're only hurting the union contractors for whom they are refusing to work. And BE&K's scabs are picking up the slack.

Frank LeClaire was among those who believed that BE&K's foray into northern Minnesota threatened the livelihood of his ironworkers and other Michigan trade union members and that the Upper Peninsula had a special stake in the strike at International Falls."

"If there's any way that I can help, name it," Frank offered.

Frank's squat frame, thick neck and flattened nose gave him the appearance of a prize fighter. His curly black hair and swarthy complexion came with his French-Canadian ancestry. His father was a commercial fisherman who thought that his only son would follow in his footsteps, but at an early age, Frank realized that he would disappoint. From his first ventures onto Lake Superior from Grand Marais, setting and lifting gill nets with his father, Frank was unable to manage the seasickness with which he was cursed. Even on those rare, calm days that settle over the lake during July and August, he would be stricken with nausea.

After stubbornly enduring his first fishing season and half of the next, Frank opted to become an apprentice ironworker. To his astonishment, he had no fear of heights and was more comfortable on a steel beam high above the ground than on the rolling deck of a Great Lakes gill net tug.

As a journeyman ironworker, Frank helped to erect some of the tallest buildings in the mid-west, including the Sears Tower in Chicago. It was there that he met and became friends with Jack Ross. They traveled together throughout much of the United States, but when work was slack, Duluth was home to Jack, and Frank returned to the Upper Peninsula. After thirty-five years as a journeyman ironworker, Frank was chosen to lead his local union.

"I have only one regret," Frank told his father. "I wish I'd been born in time to have worked with those who built the Mackinac Bridge. I can't help envying them."

As a business manager, Frank bargained effectively and rarely had to strike to get an agreement, but he never allowed his members to work alongside of non-union labor or cross another union's picket line.

It was late afternoon when Ernie arrived in Marquette. He and Frank had dinner at a restaurant on Front Street. Afterward, they climbed a narrow stairway to a large room furnished with conference tables at which trade union officers and members gathered during meetings. On this occasion, the business manager and the lawyer sat alone on metal folding chairs, facing each other across one of the ables.

The room was lighted by a row of overhead, fluorescent bulbs. At the rear wall, a pair of tall windows looked out onto a narrow alley. A floor fan barely disturbed the room's musty air while on the wall behind the two men, an expressionless Samuel Gompers watched them from a large and ornately framed photograph. A more modestly framed union charter hung next to the labor icon's portrait, and a Regulator clock's swinging pendulum ticked monotonously. The two men draped their jackets over the backs of chairs. Frank's face was flushed and moist and he rolled his shirtsleeves to his elbows. Although he was wary of lawyers, he looked to Ernie whenever he needed legal advice.

"Lawyers only want to win the argument," was Frank's complaint, "but I have to solve problems. Ernie thinks the way I do. He doesn't use a lot of fancy words and, when he talks to you, he looks you in the eye."

Ernie was of average height and build. He had straight brown hair and a small mustache that he kept neatly trimmed. Except for his mother's blue eyes and high cheekbones, his features were like those of his father and included a wide brow and square chin. His wife said that she thought of him as handsome and his demeanor made his clients feel at ease. In the courtroom, he could capture the attention of jurors and keep them focused throughout a trial.

Labor unions gave Ernie his chance to escape from the tedium of deeds and wills, the frustration of divorce and the harsh reality of criminal defense. He often lay awake at night trying to make sense of labor relations in the construction industry where a journeyman might work for a dozen different employers in a single season. Sometimes trade jurisdictions overlapped, causing rivalries among unions and conflicts between his clients. Add non-union competition to the mix and there would likely be a brawl. Nevertheless, Ernie was happy to be on the side of the working class.

"My ironworkers and other union members working on Champion's Quinnisec mill are picketing at International Falls on weekends in sympathy with union members who are on strike there," Frank told Ernie. "They think I should be involved."

"Why are the Minnesota unions striking?" Ernie asked. "What are they demanding?"

A non-union contractor was hired for the expansion of a Boise-Cascade's paper mill in International Falls. The work is being performed by scabs brought up from the South. Local union ironworkers, millwrights, pipe fitters and others are striking in protest."

Frank slid a sheet of paper across the table and waited while Ernie studied it. When Ernie passed it back, Frank continued.

"It's something I prepared as a handout," he explained. "I'm thinking of distributing it at construction sites around the UpperPeninsula. The goal is to get as many trade union members as possible to participate in a show of support for the Minnesota strike."

"So, why am I here?"

"Commercial and industrial construction has always been union in the Upper Peninsula. If the Rat can take our work from us in Minnesota, we could be it's next target."

"You haven't answered my question. Why am I here, and why do you want to take part in a strike in Minnesota? By the way, exactly whose strike is it?"

"It's a wildcat strike. I thought you would know."

"How am I supposed to know? You said it's in Minnesota. Are you also telling me it hasn't been authorized by a union?"

Frank didn't answer. Ernie continued.

"If it's a wildcat strike, why would you get involved? International Falls is hundreds of miles from here. It's outside of your jurisdiction."

"Just because Minnesota trade unions haven't authorized the strike doesn't mean that they're not in favor of it. I've been told that they're one hundred percent in sympathy."

"Sympathy doesn't count. If it's wildcat strike, it's not authorized. I'll ask again. Why do you want to get involved?"

"We can't let the Rat get a foothold on union work in Minnesota. It's too close to home."

"But if Minnesota's unions haven't stepped up to the plate…"

"Their labor agreements have 'no strike' clauses. If they strike, they will be sued. I have no agreements with Minnesota contractors. My union can't be sued if it supports the strike. My members are fired up. They have been on the picket line at International Falls and they expect me to stand with them."

"I can understand how your members might feel, but if your union takes part in a wildcat strike, it becomes your strike. What if property is damaged? What if someone gets hurt.? Do you see where I'm going with this?"

"The picketing has been peaceful. Jack Ross assured me of that."

"That's good, but you have no way of knowing what will happen tomorrow or the next day. The strike is hundreds of miles from here. You have no control of it."

"You're saying that having my union sponsor this rally is a bad idea. Is that what I'm going to have to tell my members?"

"Getting involved in a wildcat strike in another state would be like poking an electric generator with a copper rod. "

"But if I don't take a stand…"

"Your members are taking a stand. As individuals, they can walk a picket line in Michigan, Minnesota or wherever they choose. That's their right. But as the leader of their union, you take stands for the unison. our union does not do business in International Falls He his head."

"You're saying that I should stay out of it."

"That's my advice."

"I should deep six the leaflet."

"That, too, is my advice."

"I remember what you told me the first time I asked for your advice."

"I told you that you're free to ignore it, but you still have to pay for it. I tell that to all my clients. It gets them thinking about consequences."

"Well, I don't like to waste money. Got any suggestions as to how else I can support a wildcat strike without getting in trouble?"

"Not at the moment, but if I think of something I'll let you know."

"If I don't do something I'm gonna take heat from my members."

"You can count on that," barked someone standing in the doorway. He was wearing denim overalls, a sweat-stained, Green Bay Packers jersey and had a hardhat tucked under one arm. "The members have been waiting for you to take a stand. They want to know why you haven't."

"Come on in, Buck," said Frank. "Meet Ernie Hunter, our union lawyer. Ernie, meet Buck Saari, our chief steward at Quinnisec."

Ernie stood and offered his hand. Buck ignored it and took a seat next to Frank. He picked up the leaflet and studied it.

'Mind if I make some copies?" he asked.

"We won't be needing them," Frank replied. "Ernie says getting the local union involved is a bad idea."

"That doesn't mean that members can't' protest on their own," Ernie explained. "Frank tells me some have been picketing on weekends. They have that right, of course, but they shouldn't display signs or insignia that suggest the union is sponsoring them. They can display the logo of their favorite athletic team, like the one you have."

Buck did not respond. He put the leaflet back on the table. After a moment of silence, Frank stood and lifted his jacket from the back of his chair.

"I guess that wraps it," he said." Let's go over to the Shamrock and have a beer. You too, Buck."

When they reached the bottom of the stairs, Buck paused. "I'll join you in a minute," he said. "I forgot my hardhat upstairs."

Chapter Nine

At the Shamrock, a drinking establishment popular among union officers and members who gathered before and after meetings, Frank pulled a couple of chairs back from a table.

"Don't mind Buck," he told Ernie. " He takes union matters very seriously, but he means well."

The room was quiet except for the hum of an air conditioner and the murmur of conversation among the few patrons seated at the bar. Frank raised two fingers. A bartender in a white shirt and plaid vest filled two frosted mugs, brought them to the table and returned to the bar to start a tab.

"Buck can be stubborn," Frank continued. "He's got opinions and sticks to them. But I trust him and the members respect him. That's why I made him chief steward."

"What's his story beside the fact that he's a hard-nosed ironworker with opinions? How long have you known him?"

"Buck was elected to the local union executive board a year after I became the business manager. He is a militant believer in the labor movement and thinks of non-union labor as its mortal enemy."

"Where's he from?"

"He was born here in Marquette, but lived and worked in Wisconsin for a number of years. He says he always intended to return to the Upper Peninsula. When he did, he transferred into our local union."

"What about family? Is he married? Any kids?"

"He's not married. His father and mother live in town. He told me his father, who's retired, worked in the lower peninsula a long time ago. He also has a brother who's an electrician downstate.

"What kind of work did his father do?"

"'He worked in an auto plant and was in the sit-down strike at Fisher Body in Flint. That would've been in 1936, I think. After he married, he moved back to Marquette and started a family."

"You said Buck also has a brother?"

"He says his brother dodged bullets during a strike at the Essex Wire Company in Hillsdale back in 1964. Buck grew up on stories about strikes and the labor movement. He remembers hearing the explosions when railroad tracks were being blown up right here in Marquette.

How much of what he tells you do you believe?" Ernie asked. "People tend to embellish. Maybe he's got a fertile imagination."

"Maybe. But I remember the explosions, too. It happened twenty-some years ago. Maritime unions were picketing a company that shipped iron ore from here to the lower lakes. Buck would've been a teenager at the time. He says his father told him that the unions were 'kicking ass for the workin' class.' I don't recall how it ended."

Someone put money in the jukebox and Frank had to raise his voice over the sound of Patsy Cline falling to pieces.

"Buck's been going to International Falls to picket on weekends. He's got to know the strikers and I don't doubt that he is serious about wanting me to help them."

Ernie shook his head. "You don't want him getting the local union involved in someone else's fight, especially one as far away as International Falls."

"I see your point, but Buck is frustrated. While he and others are picketing, scabs keep doing what should have been union work. The way Jack Ross tells it, the strike's not even a bump in the road for BE&K. Jack keeps a low profile but he stays in touch with his striking members."

"You should keep a low profile, too, especially if there's going to be a rally. Keep an eye on Buck. He's a steward and an executive board member. What he says and does implicates the local union."

Patsy Cline stopped falling to pieces and street sounds were heard when the Shamrock's front door opened and closed. Buck strode in, pulled up a chair and put a large, rough hand on Ernie's shoulder.

"Are you buying, counsellor?"

Hank Peterson, who had been on the picket line since early in the day, began to wilt when the sun reached its zenith. By the time he finished the sandwiches he brought from home and emptied his Thermos of lemonade, his head ached. When four o'clock came, he was ready to leave.

"The years must be catching up with me," he said to Jerome as they walked together to their parked vehicles. "I need to be somewhere I can sit and rest."

Jerome, too, had been picketing most of the day and was happy to take his cue from Hank. "Let's grab a cold brew at Benny's. Meet me there and I'll buy the first round."

"I'm tempted," Hank said," but'll pass. I think I'll go to Lulu's for a coffee instead, and maybe a slice of apple pie. You sure you wouldn't rather meet me at Lulu's?"

"I don't feel like coffee. I need a shot and a beer."

"Didn't you tell me you were having problems at home? Drinking ain't gonna solve 'em."

Hank, was older than Jerome by enough years to make him feel like he was talking to a son.

"Yeah. The wife's gonna bitch at me if she smells alcohol on my breath. I ain't had a paycheck for months and she don't miss a chance to remind me. She tells me picketing is a waste of time and I tell her I got plenty'a time to waste. What choice do we have? If we weren't picketing, we'd be workin' with scabs. Maybe she thinks that's okay, but I don't. I'm gonna chill out over a drink before I go home."

"Why don't we get some coffee, instead?" Hank tried again. "I'll buy."

"Thanks, but no thanks. I might have to switch to coffee when my unemployment checks run out. Meantime, she can complain all she wants."

Hank shook his head."I'm goin' to Lulu's, or maybe I'll go on home and have my coffee. Mary should be up from her nap and she might need me."

"Go right ahead. I'm gonna see who's at Benny's. Maybe some'a them southern boys will stop by. Wouldn't that liven things up?" Jerome wondered how Hank and others would react if they knew about Hiram Pardeee.

"The southerners don't drink at Benny's," Hank reminded him. "They hang out at the Beaver Dam."

Union members shunned the Beaver Dam Bar after a newspaper account told of a brawl between some BE&K construction workers and several paper mill employees. It started over some females whose company both groups coveted. Jerome's suggestion that scabs might show up at Benny's flashed a warning signal. Hank wouldn't want to be drinking with

Jerome if scabs showed up. Jerome could be quarrelsome even when he wasn't drinking.

The two men got into their vehicles and Hank drove south on 8th Avenue. In his rear view mirror, he saw Jerome's Chevy pickup turn east onto 2nd Street. At that moment, a black Buick sedan pulled in behind Hank's Ford Bronco, almost touching its rear bumper.

Hank had seen Alderton's guards driving Buick sedans, most of which were black. He stepped on his accelerator and the Bronco lurched forward and accelerated. He made a sudden right turn onto 3rd Street. The Buick followed. Hank made a left onto 9th Avenue and another left at 4th Street. The Buick stayed close. At the end of the block on 4th, he made a right turn back onto 8th Avenue and at 5th Street he made another sharp turn and braked to a sudden stop. The Buick stopped behind him and waited. Hank's turn signal continued to flash until oncoming traffic cleared, allowing him to turn left into the parking lot of the International Falls Law Enforcement Building. The Buick's tires squealed as it accelerated and sped eastward on 5th, disappearing around the corner at the end of the block.

Tyrone had noticed Hank on the picket line earlier in the day. What he saw was someone slightly stooped and older than others who were picketing. Hank shuffled although he managed to keep up. Tyrone wondered what an old geezer like Hank was doing on a picket line. He thought that Hank walked like a pigeon, or maybe more like a duck, not like someone you'd see on a picket line. But it was obvious that Hank was with the union, which made him a thug.

Later, when Tyrone was sitting behind the wheel of the Buick, ready to return to his motel, he watched Hank hoist himself into the Bronco. That was when Tyrone made the spur of the moment decision to follow Hank. He had no particular purpose or plan in mind except the thought that it might be fun to throw a scare into the old man. It might add a bit of excitement to what had been a very dull day. Tyrone's morning was spent checking BE&K workers through the gate while the picketing strikers jeered. He and the other guards had to make several sweeps for roofing nails and a few fenders and door panels were gouged. Tyrone could hear the screech of metal on metal, but he couldn't see what was being used to make gouges— keys, he assumed. Each time it happened, his pulse quickened, but before he could react, the strikers would move away and join the slow, monotonous parade outside the fence. The rest of Tyrone's day was punctuated by insults, obscenities and threats as strikers and guards tried to outdo each other between lapses of indifference.

Tyrone wished he could challenge these men who mocked him and showed no respect for the people or property he was protecting. He felt like he needed to punch someone, but had to shrug it off. He was bigger than most of the men on the picket line, and he had a baton and a flashlight, but they were too many and the other guards at the gate were questionable assets. One was fat and had tattoos and long, shaggy hair. Another chain-smoked cigarettes and read girly magazines in the guard shack. Tyrone hoped that he wouldn't have to rely on either of them in a fight with the strikers.

When Tyrone came within inches of the Bronco's rear bumper, he could almost feel Hank's panic as the older man tried to out-maneuver the Buick. By the time both vehicles came to a stop across from the parking lot, Tyrone thought that Hank must be sweating. In the parking lot, Hank sat with the engine running and considered whether he should file a complaint. He didn't get a close look, but he was certain the driver was one of the guards from the construction site. Would he be able to pick him out of a lineup? What lineup? Was there a crime or was he just a frightened old man with an overactive imagination? He released his grip on the door handle, slipped from Park into Drive and rolled slowly from the parking lot into the street. What he wanted most was to be at home having a cup of coffee with Mary.

Several blocks away, Tyrone smiled to himself thinking that he would tell the guys that he chased a union thug all the way from the construction site to the cop shop's parking lot. He would say that he scared the crap out of him and would tell them how the guy must have given the cops an earful before they laughed and told him, "Sorry, but no harm, no foul." He turned the car radio on and drummed his fingers on the steering wheel to the beat of Michael Jackson's "Bad".

Chapter Ten

After Jerome downed his first shot of Jameson, he turned away from the bar to face the men sitting at tables behind him. A few were trade union members with whom he picketed earlier in the day. Others belonged to the millworkers union. It was payday for Boise-Cascade employees, and the pitchers of beer were paid for by the men who worked in the mill.

"Hey, Jerry," one of the construction workers called out, pointing to an empty chair," come sit with us. We want your opinion."

Jerome grabbed his beer and slid off his stool.

"What's up?"

"Sit and tell us how we can get rid of BE&K's scabs. Picketing is getting us nowhere because we can't lay a hand on the scabs and they know it. The law's on their side and we're just putting on a show. So, what's the answer? Is there a plan B?"

Jerome glanced at Debbie, wondering if she told anyone about the drink he had with the southerner. Debbie shook her head, not because she read his thoughts, but because she had heard their complaints over and over, beginning with her husband who left town before the strike was a week old.

"I ain't gonna waste my time on a picket line that's not gonna change a thing," he told her. "Anyone who thinks they can win this strike can stay here and picket all they want. I'm going to be where there's work to be had."

Debbie remembered what life was like years earlier when her father walked a picket line, to get a contract at the mill. The strike went on for months and he never fully recovered the wages he lost. But the union got a contract and it included better pay and benefits. That strike was about the right to organize.This strike was about giving local jobs to strangers who never had a labor contract and didn't know what it cost her father's generation to get one.

"Back in the day," Jerome was saying, "we would' have done whatever was necessary to run a bunch of scabs off of a job."

"Meaning what?" Debbie asked. "Do you think you can scare them? They came from hundreds of miles away because they need the work as much as you and maybe more."

"We'll think of something," Jerome said. "You'll see."

"While I'm waiting, who's buying?" she asked.

The mill workers got up. Others took it as their cue and followed them out. Jerome returned to the bar with his unfinished beer. Debbie sighed as she began to clear tables and pick up a few coins and a dollar bill.

It was almost midnight when Officer Joel Carmody found Jerome in an alley behind a home rented to several BE&K construction workers, one of whom had called in a complaint. A bedroom window at the rear of the home was shattered, another was cracked and Jerome was sprawled against a wire fence that guarded a small back yard. He appeared to be sleeping. On closer inspection he reeked of alcohol.

Carmody recognized Jerome from a previous encounter involving a domestic violence complaint. Jerome came home drunk and spoiling for a fight. He awakened his wife with a punch to the side of her head and threatened to "kick her ass" if she didn't tell him where she hid his bottle of bourbon. By the time Carmody arrived, Jerome was passed out on the living room couch and his wife was sitting in a rocker with an ice pack pressed to her cheek. She declined to press charges, but promised that when Jerome sobered up she would "take care of the bastard" herself. Carmody did not ask her to elaborate.

In the alley behind the damaged home, it was the renters whose sleep had been disturbed by rocks striking glass and the sound of glass shattering that wanted to "take care of" Jerome. Carmody declined the offer, settling instead for some less than gentle assistance to hoist Jerome into the rear of the officer's patrol car.

Carmody was unable to elicit an intelligible explanation for Jerome's presence in the alley, but he did not doubt that his inebriated passenger was at least partly responsible the damaged windows. He could not say for certain that it was Jerome who threw rocks. Others could have been involved. But if here were others, they fled the scene before the officer arrived. He would charge Jerome with public intoxication. It would be up to the county attorney to decide whether to charge a more serious offense. Jerome could not be accused of resisting arrest. He was in no shape for that.

When the late news ended, Hank turned off the television and went to bed. Mary was snoring lightly. Several blocks away, a pickup truck with out-of-state license plates was tipped over on its side. The tires of several other out-of-state vehicles parked nearby were slashed and several homes in the neighborhood were pelted with eggs and rocks. Hank learned of the vandalism the next day while watching the morning news. He decided to stay home and spend the day with Mary. She was pleased.

In the morning, Police Chief David Patterson and Sheriff Harold Noonan, were not pleased when they finished reviewing the incident reports they received from their night-duty officers and deputies. They described something likened to a nocturnal war.

"BE&K's people are being targeted," the Chief said. The threats being made on the picket line leave little room for doubt as to who's behind this rash of vandalism."

"It's not entirely one-sided," the Sheriff countered. "The strikers have been complaining that they've been threatened and some of their vehicles have been damaged. Their fingers are pointed at the security guards who the say are stalking them when they leave the picket line. Seems we have a bit of tit for tat on our hands."

"My officers are able to keep an eye on BE&K's work crews as they go in and come out during the day," Patterson said. "But most of the trouble has been occurring at night, after the bars close. The arson has me more worried than anything else that has happened. It could have had deadly consequences. We need more officers patrolling at night "

"I agree," Noonan replied, "but I have a jail to run, and I can only assign my road patrol deputies to as much overtime as my budget will allow. That leaves me with limited options at night."

Noonan was a retired Minneapolis police detective who, after returning to his home town, was elected Koochiching County Sheriff and re-elected for two more consecutive terms, thanks in part the support of the unions whose members were on strike.

"The men on the picket line believe they are the victims. I suppose I might feel that way, too, if I were in their shoes. But that's not an excuse for lawlessness. I'd like to believe that the vandalism is the work of outside agitators. Outsiders have no stake in the community. It's the out-of-state element that worries me most."

"The strike's sympathizers are here only on weekends," Patterson said. "We can't ignore the likelihood that it's local citizens that are involved in the incidents that have been occurring during the week."

The Chief, tall, blond and somewhat boyish looking, was a transplant from Grafton, North Dakota. Younger than the Sheriff, he looked to the older man for advice. He was a strict believer in the law, but he faulted Boise-Cascade for hiring southern labor.

"I can't say that much good has come from bringing BE&K to town, but if local citizens are committing crimes, they have be held accountable."

"My report says that your officers brought a couple of prisoners to my jail last night," the sheriff said. "What was that about?"

"Another bar fight at the Beaver Dam. Over a woman. That's usually how it starts. I'll let you know when formal complaints are ready so that your deputies can bring the combatants to court for arraignment later this morning. And there was a property damage arrest, too. The report indicates that the suspect was feeling no pain when he was apprehended at the scene."

"I was about to ask about him," the sheriff said. "He was booked into the jail around midnight. He's still sleeping it off in the drunk tank. Where did your officers find him?"

"Officer Carmody found him in an alley. He was passed out behind a home that had some windows broken. We can get him arraigned, too, when the paperwork's sent over by the county attorney, that is, if he can stand and walk by then. I mean the suspect, not the county attorney."

While Patterson and Noonan were comparing notes, Jerome was awakening to the shuffling and muttering of prisoners in the jail cell next to the drunk tank. He also was experiencing spasms of nausea as he tried to remember how he came to be curled up on a lumpy, foul smelling mattress instead of the king-size Beautyrest that he shared with his wife when they weren't feuding. He shuddered at the thought of his wife who would demand to know where he'd been. He tried to think of an explanation she might accept, but his head ached and his mind kept returning to Benny's Saloon and the men buying drinks. It had been payday at the mill which is why he decided to go to Benny's, but he could not remember leaving.

He sat up and felt a stabbing pain behind his eyes. When he closed them, Debbie was pouring shots. He tried to bring her into focus but she remained blurred like the faces at the table. He could not remember where he had been after he left the saloon. As he sat on the lumpy mattress and rubbed his eyes, a

synapse pierced the fog clouding his brain and he saw himself struggling with a uniformed officer. Maybe it was two officers. Red and blue lights were flashing when he was shoved into the rear seat of a police cruiser with his face pressed against a metal screen.

Jerome did not recall the ride in the patrol car, but he remembered the sound of a metal door that slammed shut behind him as he was pushed or he fell onto a cot. It must have been the same one on which he was now sitting, half awake and fully dressed, with no blanket. His bare feet were on a cold cement floor. He was shivering. His shoes. Where were his shoes? He leaned forward, elbows on his knees, and pressed his fingers against his temples. It didn't stop the pain in his head. When he raised up and tried to look around, it got worse. He had no doubt as to where he was, but didn't know what he was going to tell his wife when he got home.

Jerome was arraigned and released from custody later that morning after promising that he would not flee the jurisdiction of the court. Red-eyed, disheveled and not knowing where he left his car, he made the long walk home, dreading the inevitable confrontation. His wife would demand an explanation and he could not think of one that was both innocent and credible. When he reached his front door, it wasn't locked. He entered and called her name softly, as if she might be sleeping. Hearing no answer, he went to the bottom of the stairway to their bedroom and called to her once more. No response. He shouted her name and waited. Nothing. In the kitchen, on the table, he found a note in his wife's neat hand:

"I'm at mother's. Get a job."

Chapter Eleven

A noisy poker game kept Hiram awake during much of his second night in a smoke-filled man camp trailer. Fretting over the money he had spent at Benny's the night before, he declined separate invitations to get in on the action and to join several other trailer-mates for drinks at the Beaver Dam Bar. There would be no poker games and no more saloons. Hiram was a family man even if he was not able to live like one.

Man camp occupants were either single or left families behind. They came from places where few employers offered wages comparable to what they were paid by BE&K. They were in International Falls for the money and were determined to stay as long as there was money to be made. The jeers and curses that greeted them them when they crossed the picket line were like the weather. Work went on, rain or shine.

Hiram left the man camp on a company bus in the morning and returned on the bus at the end of the day. He was neither for or against the men who were picketing. He was there to do the job for which the company was paying him. The strike belonged to a world in which he was a temporary visitor. That his presence was the reason for the strike did not cause him concern, and if he happened to see Jerome on the picket line, he would look the other away.

Hiram didn't smoke but a constant blue haze hovered over the men in the trailer and he accepted the offer of a cigarette as a gesture of fellowship. Although Betsy had lectured him about his diet, he felt obliged to cough up a dollar and some change for a share of pizza that proved to be less than what he needed to satisfy his hunger. A second cigarette might have helped, but he didn't ask. Betsy had also cautioned against developing bad habits. He was about to fall asleep when the group that went to the Beaver Dam returned. Pressing himself against the wall next to his bunk, he pulled a pillow over his head. It was no use.

In his motel room a few miles from the man camp, Tyrone was telling how he terrorized a "union thug."

When I chased him into the parking lot, he jumped out and ran like a scared rabbit." He chose "rabbit" over "duck" although neither conveyed the image he wanted.

"Was it the old guy who drives a Bronco?" someone asked, "You're lucky he didn't kick your butt."

Tyrone ignored the snickers. "Very funny. Fact is I scared the crap out'a him. He was about to have a stroke. "

"But you let him get away."

"Was I supposed to follow him into a building full of cops?"

"You could've told the desk sergeant you were horny and needed directions to the nearest whorehouse."

The laughter followed Tyrone down the hall to a fitness center where he stripped to the waist and settled onto a weight bench. He found a rhythm and began counting his lifts until his muscles ached and sweat was running from his armpits. When he was satisfied, he stood, picked up his shirt and carried it back to his room where he finished undressing and showered. Afterward, he put on pajamas and slipped into a robe. Sitting on the bed with a remote and with pillows tucked behind him, he turned the television on. The lead news story was about the ongoing investigation of a house fire and a family that was left homeless. Arson was believed to be the cause, but no suspects were in custody. It was stale news. By the time the weather report came on, Tyrone was sleeping.

Officer Carmody's shift began with a trouble call from the Beaver Dam Bar where an argument between several Alderton Security guards and BE&K construction workers prompted a bartender's plea for help. The guards, having mistaken the workers for "union thugs," tried to goad them into a bare knuckle test of manliness.
A male chorus of dixie drawls exposed the error. By the time Carmody arrived, the guards were watching the replay of a baseball game's highlights on a television screen mounted above the bar. The BE&K men were casting salacious looks at a group of women. They were being ignored because the women were eyeballing the guards who were in uniform.

Inside the doorway, Carmody made a visual assessment, preparing to act if needed. A few of the guards looked familiar, but he didn't recognize any of the men at the other tables. He studied the women. Their gaudy outfits made it apparent that they were not local. The bartender was busy mixing drinks and had his back turned. No one appeared to be in distress.

"Can we buy you a drink, officer?" asked one of the guards.

"I'm on duty, but thanks just the same. Maybe some other time."

The guards ordered a round "for the ladies," and the BE&K men watched while the bartender served the drinks. When "the ladies" raised their glasses and saluted their benefactors, the BE&K men lost interest. The guards returned to watching television and the officer could see no reason to stay.

Outside, the air was cool and the noise from the bar was muted. Carmody got into his patrol car and continued his rounds, stopping an hour later to eat the sandwich he brought from home. The coffee in his Thermos was sweet and hot. He had one other trouble call. It brought him to an alley and a house that had been pelted with rocks. He made an arrest and delivered an inebriated suspect to the jail. When he wrote his report, his shift ended.

When Carmody arrived home, his twin ten year old sons were leaving for the school playground. The baseball season that began shortly after classes let out in June was about to end. Their team was in second place, but they still had a chance to be in first. They squirmed in their father's affectionate grasp and were out the door the moment they were free.

"They think they're too old for hugs," Carmody complained to his wife.

"They have baseball on their minds."

"I know," he sighed, "and I wanted to watch them play today, but I spent the last hour of my shift wrestling a drunk and I need to get some sleep."

He collapsed onto his recliner and began to remove his shoes. "Maybe we can watch them play tomorrow," he offered. "The season is almost over, and they're not out of the running for the league championship. We should be there for them."

She pulled a chair next to him. "I don't know if I'm up for another game. It's not fun anymore, the way it used to be."

"What's that supposed to mean?"

"When the season began, local moms and dads and BE&K parents simply ignored each other."

"That's because we sat at opposite ends of the bleachers," he reminded her. "We cheered for our kids and they cheered for theirs."

"That's right," she said, "and everything was calm until the cheers got louder and the wisecracks and insults got mixed in. The adults set a terrible example."

"I guess it's been a while since I watched them play," he said. "I wasn't aware. Tomorrow we'll go together."

"I'm afraid that sooner or later a fight will break out and I don't want to be there when it happens. You told me there was a fight among some teenagers in the park and you said there have been bar fights. It scares me, all this anger and resentment."

"It's mostly young males being macho, trying to show how tough they are. It's not something that should keep us from watching a ball game. I'm not on duty tomorrow, but I'll wear my uniform. Nobody will bother us."

"Have we come to where we need uniformed police at a children's game? It never used to be like this. Why can't people get along?"

"Folks who've been here all their lives, especially those that are barely getting by on unemployment checks, feel they're being cheated. Some are watching their savings disappear. Some had to leave the area to find work while strangers stay here and put in forty hours a week."

She stood and faced him. "They say the new mill won't be finished for at least another year. Something needs to be done now."

"Some of the hardship may be unavoidable, but the mill's expansion will eventually mean jobs that will be filled locally. That's something to look forward to."

"I've heard all that, but why should I have to be afraid to go downtown to shop or go to a ball park to watch our children play?"

"It's not only us. It's difficult for the southerners, too. I'm not talking about broken windows and bar fights. A family is homeless because the house they were renting was set on fire. Ño one was injured, but others may not be as lucky if it happens again."

"That's why it has to stop."

"We're doing what we can. I made an arrest this morning—a drunk in an alley. He was behind a house with broken windows. I also answered a call to a bar fight. Fortunately, it was a false alarm. We're getting calls from people just because they think someone's looking at them the wrong way."

"Do you have any idea who set the fire?"

"Not yet."

"Could it have been the person you arrested in the alley this morning?"

"I suppose that's possible, but I don't have any evidence that it was him. I dealt with him one other time, but to say he might be our arsonist would be pure speculation."

"Do you think that it's someone from town?"

"It could be anyone."

She lifted his uniform jacket from his lap. I'll hang this up while you change clothes."

"I'm comfortable as is. I'll shower and slip into my jeans after I nap. Maybe this afternoon you, me and the boys can go for a ride somewhere. We could go to a park and have a picnic. How's that sound?"

He eased the recliner back. By the time she returned from putting his jacket away, he was asleep.

Hank Peterson spread a blanket on the grass where he and Mary could watch and listen to children laugh and squeal as they slid to the ground and rushed to climb the metal steps to the top of the slide again. Hank cleared thoughts of the picket line from his mind and the afternoon sun brought a bit of color to Mary's cheeks.

"A breath of fresh air is just what I needed," she exclaimed. "Watching the children reminds me of the playgrounds of my own childhood. Some things never change."

Hank had been picketing, never less than four hours and often more, almost every day since the strike began. The strike seemed to have lost whatever importance it might have had in the beginning when everyone believed it would force Boise-Cascade to replace BE&K with a union-friendly contractor.

"I never liked strikes," he told Mary, "although I know that something has to be done to keep scabs from taking union work. This strike troubles me more than most. It wasn't called by a union and it isn't stoping the scabs."

Hank had asked Jack Ross why the unions weren't trying to organize the scabs "Shouldn't they have to pay dues and wait their turn for work like the rest of us?"

"If we were to take the scabs into the union and make them pay dues, I would have to put them on our work list and find jobs for them."

"What's wrong with that?" Hank asked.

"How am I supposed to find jobs for scabs when there ain't enough jobs for the members we already have? Think about it. Do you want to add all those good old boys from Alabama or Mississippi or wherever else they come from to our work list? And if they were eligible to vote in our elections, I'd be gone and so would the entire executive board, not to mention our job stewards. We would stop being a Minnesota union."

Hank wasn't entirely satisfied by Jack's answer, but he didn't have a better one. He needed to give it more thought, but not while he and Mary were enjoying a picnic in Smokey Bear Park.

"Let's look for a shady spot under a tree," she said. "Forget about the union and the strike and let's enjoy our sandwiches."

She had packed a lunch at home, thinking that when they were hungry, they would find a picnic table and cover it with their blanket. When they finished eating, they found a grassy spot and spread their blanket in some shade. The sun was lower and there was a cool breeze coming from the north. It was still daylight when they grew tired of watching children play.

"Maybe you can stay home tomorrow, too," Mary suggested as they prepared to leave.

"Maybe," Hank replied.

Chapter Twelve

As a chief steward, Buck could circulate freely among the ironworkers at Quinnisec, which also brought him into frequent contact with union members who belonged to other trades. While he handed out copies of a leaflet promoting a labor union rally in Minnesota, he was filling a shopping bag with donations—five, ten and, even a few twenty dollar bills to pay for a bus to International Falls.

"Stop right there," a voice demanded over the din of work. "Hand those over."

Pete Hazeltine, the Quinnisec project's construction superintendent, snatched a few leaflets from Buck's grasp.

"It's my responsibility as chief steward to keep the members informed," Buck said, shifting the bag filled with donations behind his back. "You got a problem with that?"

"Your duties don't include disrupting work. Do your leafleting on your own time or you'll be chief steward at the unemployment office."

The two men glared at each other while others stood by and watched. Buck, taller and heavier of the two, fought an urge to swat the smaller man if only to save face. But Hazeltine, who could hire and fire, was showing no fear; and Buck was hesitant to demand that Pete give back the leaflets he had grabbed because nothing had been said about the bag with the money. The moment passed and Hazeltine turned and walked away, still clutching the leaflets. Buck gave a wink and a thumbs up to those who had been watching and he left the area, still holding the bag.

For those who had witnessed it, Buck's encounter with Hazeltine was the high point of the day. When the day ended, they followed the chief steward to Iron Mountain to begin the weekend with beer, pickled eggs and venison sausage.

"Hey Buck. How come you let Pete get away with your leaflets? You're bigger than him. Why didn't you knock him on his ass?

"No big deal," Buck growled. "I can get more leaflets."

One of the men had a leaflet stuffed into a shirt pocket. He withdrew it and read it again before handing it across the table to a pipefitter.

"Have you seen one of these?"

"Yeah," he said, handing it to the bartender. "Take a look in case you're off next weekend and have nothing better to do."

The bartender put the leaflet on the table.

"I'm workin' next weekend. I work every weekend. This ain't a union shop. But I'm with you guys all the way."

An ironworker picked up the leaflet and waved it at Buck. "Does this mean Frank LeClaire has finally seen the light. Why'd he wait so long to get on board?"

"Frank's the cautious type," Buck said.

"Will he be on the bus?"

Before Buck could answer, someone else asked, "Do you have enough to pay for the bus? If you need me to lean on anyone for more, just say the word." He was as tall as Buck, but heavier.

"I haven't had time to count it," Buck replied, "but I'm sure there's enough for at least one bus, maybe two."

"How many do you expect will be going?" the big man asked.

"I'll take a head count next week. If there's more than fifty, some will have to car pool or we'll need a second bus."

"If you need a second bus," the big man said, "some of the union members who are working in Wisconsin and lower Michigan will be home for Labor Day. I'll hit them up for donations."

Pete Hazeltine picked up his phone and dialed. He thought that Mike Carr at International Falls should know about the leaflet. Carr, who was Pete's boss when the two worked at a construction project in Escanaba, picked up his phone even though he was preparing to leave for the long, Labor Day weekend. Pete transferred to the Quinnisec project when the Escanaba job was finished. Mike was recruited by BE&K to be its superintendent at International Falls. During the months that followed, the two stayed in touch by telephone. When Mike told Pete about the wildcat strike, Mike said it was "a fool's errand," predicting that it would be short-lived and that the Boise-Cascade expansion would be completed on schedule. Pete wasn't as sanguine as Mike.

"I have the leaflet in my hand," he . "I don't know how many copies were passed out, but anyone who didn't get one is sure to hear about it. The ironworkers are urging all union members working here to take part in this so-called rally. You might want to find out where else the leaflet is being distributed. There's union construction in Milwaukee and Chicago, too."

And in Bloomington," Mike added. "I also heard that the Minnesota Building Trades Council is planning a demonstration at the state capitol in St. Paul on September 16. They want to protest the state's support of Boise-Cascade's expansion."

"I thought that Minnesota's unions weren't supporting the strike."

"That was my understanding, too. Jack Ross insists that the strike isn't authorized. I don't know why the Building Trades Council is getting involved."

"All I know from the leaflet is that Michigan ironworkers are sponsoring an event in International Falls on September 9," Pete said. "I thought I should let you know as soon as possible."

"Thanks for the heads-up. If large numbers of people are coming here from out-of-state, that's a formula for trouble. FAX a copy of the leaflet to me and I'll pass it on to BE&K's corporate chain of command. Boise-Cascade has a contract with a security company. It might be prudent to ask for more protection."

"I hope I haven't spoiled your weekend."

"I heard rumors earlier in the week, but they were the kind you're always likely to hear during a strike. I guess I should have taken time to follow up. Now that you've given me something more substantial, I'll sound an alarm. We have a week to get ready."

"Is your project still on schedule?" Pete asked. "The last time we spoke, you said that there'd been some vandalism?"

"The serious stuff happens off-site where there's no security and not much of a police presence. But nothing has happened to slow the work and we're right on schedule."

When the call ended, Pete slid the leaflet into the FAX tray, dialed and waited. Four rings later, the leaflet began its slide.

Ernie Hunter loved challenges. In law school, the challenge was learning to ask the right questions. He also learned that correct answers can disappoint. Justice usually depends upon which side you are on.

After passing his Bar examination, Ernie was hired by a large, urban law firm. Unwilling to languish as the junior associate in a long line of associates waiting to become partners, he closed his briefcase, packed his suitcase and moved to the Upper Peninsula. From a modestly-appointed office in Escanaba, he defended clients charged with drunk driving, simple assault, petty theft, poaching and other minor offenses and an occasional felony. He kept his fees in a range his clients could afford, and, from time to time, a gift of contraband venison or illegally netted fish supplemented his income. His career plateaued until Frank LeClaire introduced him to the idiosyncrasies of labor law.

Several of the contractors with whom Frank's union had agreements demanded to be released from an ancient promise they had made to only hire ironworkers who were members of Frank's union. These "closed shop" agreements were negotiated long before Frank became business manager, and long before the law declared them to be illegal. They had ceased to be enforced, but the language remained in the agreements and Frank could think of no persuasive argument to counter the demand that it be removed. To make matters worse, some of his members objected to the contractors' demand,. Frank needed cover.

"The contractors have a valid point," Ernie told him. "There is no legal justification for keeping the language in your agreements. Refusing to delete it may result in an unfair labor practice charge. The labor board will rule in the contractors favor a.. I advise you to remove the language and be done with the matter."

"The lawyer says the language is illegal," Frank told his members at a union meeting. "He says it must go."

There was some grumbling and an ironworker at the rear of the hall stood and asked to be recognized.

"Tell the lawyer that we pay him to put language into our agreements," he demanded. "We don't pay him to take language out."

Although his secretary left the office for the weekend, Frank stayed behind making telephone calls to remind ironworkers that Monday's Labor Day parade would begin assembling at nine o'clock in the morning. Once every year, the parade put the tiny, Upper Peninsula village of Rock on the map and union participation was a mainstay of the tradition. Frank expected every available ironworker to meet him at the staging area where they would join other union members from across the peninsula.

Miles away in Minnesota, Jack Ross looked forward to spending the long weekend at home In Duluth. His wife insisted on it. For months, Edith had watched her husband fret over the strike at International Falls.

"You told them it was a bad idea from the very beginning," she reminded him. "If they didn't listen, why should you keep beating yourself up over it? When they get tired of picketing, the strike will end and it will be forgotten."

"I feel I'm being disloyal by sitting it out, " he explained, even though she had heard it before. "The strike may be doomed, but how else can they protest what they see as an injustice? That's how Frank LeClaire sees it, too."

"How did Frank get dragged into it ? BE&K hasn't taken any work from Michigan's ironworkers?"

"His members are worried that non-union contractors will bid for work in Michigan. They're planning a rally at International Falls the Saturday after Labor Day. "

"What good will that do?"

"Who knows? It probably won't change anything, but it might boost morale."

"Then why get worked up over it? Forget International Falls for a few days. Let's enjoy the holiday. You can start worrying again next week."

Chapter Thirteen

Rachel Hunter, a tall, statuesque Scandinavian blonde with pale green eyes and a deep voice, fascinated Ernie from the day they met. She had a mocking smile that delighted him even when she rejected his clumsy attempts to seduce her.

"You're married to the law," she told him. "I'm just a diversion. When your tired of me, you'll look for someone else to amuse you."

Hoping to convince her that she misjudged him, Ernie courted her with unwavering determination, even accompanying her to auctions, flea markets and rummage sales where, holding up an item for which Ernie could only hope to guess its purpose, she might say, "This is something I simply cannot live without."

Why not? " he might ask, regretting his ignorance.

"My grandmother had one. I might never find another like it."

"Give me a hint. What's it used for?"

"It's for stuffing sausages. Can't you tell?"

"Of course. How could I not know. But what will you do with it?"

"I might take up charcuterie."

Although he didn't know what "charcuterie," was, he enjoyed her riddles and surprises and she kept him amply supplied with both. She had a keen eye for value and rarely passed up a bargain. She called them "undiscovered treasures."

When they married, Rachel made it her mission to find a hobby for Ernie. She bought him a camera. His photographs were put into a drawer and forgotten. She gave him her stamp collection. It joined the photographs. She continued to take him to antique shops, flea markets and rummage sales and he became her pupil.

Ahead of Monday's Labor Day parade in Rock, they attended the annual antique gas and steam engine show at the Escanaba Fairgrounds. Neither of them had any interest in old machinery, but the flea market that accompanied the event lured Rachel and Ernie tagged along. Moments after they arrived, Rachel discovered a wide-brimmed, straw hat with a pink bow and ribbon. She thought it resembled something her mother might have worn. Holding it up so that Ernie and others nearby could see, she set it on her head and tilted the brim at an angle that shaded one eye while she winked with the other.

"Do you like it?" she asked.

"A perfect fit. You can wear it to tomorrow's parade," he replied, thinking that afterward, it would probably join the photographs and stamps.

Looking beyond her and studying the crowd, Ernie's gaze came upon a familiar face. Their eyes met and it was too late to pretend they hadn't seen each other. Buck was standing near an antiquated steam engine that he was no longer inspecting because he had taken notice of the tall blonde that seemed to belong to Ernie. Buck was waiting for them to move on.

"Do you need money for the hat?" Ernie asked.

Before she could respond, he was making his way through the crowds gathered around flea market tables while Rachel watched with her prize perched on her head.

"I didn't know you were interested in ancient machinery," he said when he reached Buck.

He extended his hand. This time, Buck took it.

"It's just something to fill my time," Buck said. "I'm off work until Tuesday and there's not much else happening before tomorrow's parade. Will you and your lady be there?"

"We haven't decided, yet. It depends on the weather. Will you be marching?"

"I always do. You wanna march with us? Your lady is welcome to march with us, too."

"Her name is Rachel. I'll ask her. Are you still planning to hold a rally in Minnesota next week?"

"It's all set."

"Your mind is made up."

"Yep."

"I hope it goes well, but keep in mind that it's not union-sponsored. It's individuals that are protesting."

"Got it."

Ernie tried to think of something more persuasive, but nothing came to mind.

"When you see Frank, say 'Hi' for me."

"Be at the parade and say it yourself, counselor."

They shook hands again and Ernie returned to Rachel who was still wearing the hat.

"You owe me five bucks," she said.

Under a cloudless Labor Day sky, people lined both sides of the highway that runs through the village of Rock. Some brought folding chairs. Others sat on blankets. A few shielded themselves from the sun with umbrellas. As the parade passed them, children darted onto the pavement to retrieve wrapped candies tossed from floats pulled by tractors and pickup trucks. Cheers and applause greeted a company of flag-bearing veterans dressed in outdated, ill-fitting uniforms. Political incumbents and candidates seeking to replace them criss-crossed the highway on foot, shaking hands, handing out literature and stopping now and then to chat with constituents. Local merchants in placard-bearing vehicles were followed by senior citizens on motorcycles, teens on horseback and children on bicycles. Marching bands from nearby high schools provided the cadence to which the unions' rank and file marched.

At the picnic area where the crowd would gather after the parade, food vendors waited in their tents and the aroma of hotdogs, bratwurst and burgers on charcoal grills began to fill the air. A pair of electric guitars, a keyboard and drums were warming up when Buck and Frank entered the beer tent. Ernie took Rachel's hand and led her to where they had parked before the parade began.

"Why such a hurry to leave?" She asked. I was looking forward to a bratwurst or maybe a pasty and a beer."

"We can grab a bite later," he told her. "I don't want to get tied up with Frank LeClaire and Buck, the guy I spoke with yesterday at the flea market."

She was silent during the ride home.

"You must have known that Frank would be at the parade," she said when they were sitting at the kitchen table. "Didn't you know that Buck would be there, too?"

"I knew they'd both be there, but I also know there's some friction between them and I don't care to be involved."

"Frank's your client. I thought the two of you were on good terms. Is there a problem?"

"If there is a problem, it's not with Frank. I'm not sure about Buck."

She opened a can of something and put slices of bread on a plate.

"While I'm doing this," she said, "get the mayo out of the fridge and, while you're up, you can get me a beer."

"Buck's been pressuring Frank to get involved in the strike at International Falls. I told Frank that I thought he should stay out of it. I think Buck is resentful. I didn't want to get into an argument at the parade, and definitely not in the beer tent."

She set their plates on the table. He opened a beer and passed it to her.

"I've given Frank my advice. It's up to him to deal with Buck."

"Are you worried that Buck will get Frank to ignore your advice?"

"Frank is free to ignore my advice if he chooses."

"I know," she sighed, "but he still has to pay for it. Right?"

Labor Day at International Falls included a kiddie parade, baseball games and fireworks. A small number of pickets kept a quiet vigil at BE&K's construction gate. In the city parks, more than the usual number of police officers were on duty and wary BE&K families gathered at prudent distances from local families. Lulu's Cafe was closed for the day, allowing Wanda to sleep late and spend the afternoon tidying up her small apartment. Nobody stopped for drinks at Benny's, and Debbie stacked chairs on tables and mopped the floor before locking up early and going home. The Beaver Dam was busy throughout the day and continued to rock into the night. Hiram Pardee spent the weekend in the man camp, watching sitcom reruns, late-night movies, and twenty-four hour cable news. When morning arrived, law enforcement breathed a collective sigh of relief.

Early on Tuesday, Mike Carr placed a telephone call to BE&K's corporate office in Birmingham, Alabama.

"I faxed the leaflet to you about half an hour ago," he told Harlan Dixon. "I received it at the end of the day on Friday. I thought you should have it on your desk first thing this morning."

"I've already spoken with Boise-Cascade's mill manager," BE&K's senior vice president replied. "He's going to contact Alderton Security and I'm going to turn the matter over to a lawyer."

"Do you have someone in your legal department who's dealt with mass picketing? I don't imagine that happens very often in Alabama?"

"Forget Alabama. Our in-house legal staff would have trouble finding International Falls on a map. I want someone who's familiar with Minnesota."

"I can make a few inquiries if you'd like."

"That won't be necessary. I already have someone in mind. He has experience in labor matters and he won't be swayed by local politics."

"Is there anything else I can do?"

"I intend to be on the first flight to Minneapolis tomorrow morning. I'm meeting with the lawyer at two o'clock in the afternoon. I want you to be there."

"What's the address?"

"I'll put my secretary on the phone. She'll give you directions and she can make arrangements for lodging if you decide to fly down today."

"That won't be necessary. I'll get an early start in the tomorrow morning and drive down. If anyone from Boise-Cascade will be joining us, perhaps we can share the ride."

"Boise's mill manager declined my invitation. It's going to be you, me and the lawyer."

Royce Gunderson, Boise's mill manager, could think of no good reason to get involved in a dispute between BE&K and the trade unions. The mill's hourly workers were already in a surly mood over concessions their union had to make in order to get a contract and bring an end to a lengthy and contentious negotiation.

"Our mill employees are cheering for the strikers," Gunderson told Dixon, "but they haven't walked out in sympathy. As long as the mill is producing, I'm not going to do anything that might provoke them."

Gunderson placed a telephone call to Alderton Security's Seymour Hoekstra, who tried to make a case for more guards at the construction site.

"You already have a small paramilitary force in place," Gunderson reminded him. "Crowd control is the responsibility of the police department. We pay taxes for that."

"The local cops might not have enough manpower to control an unruly mob," Hoekstra persisted.

Gunderson cut him off. "Maybe it's time for BE&K to accept some of the burden of providing security. You can pass that on at tomorrow's meeting in Minneapolis. I won't be there."

Dixon had told Hoekstra that he was welcome to attend the meeting by telephone. "You can call in at two in the afternoon, Central Time. The lawyer's name is Conrad Jorgensen. He's with Peters, Smythe, Jorgensen and Jones in the Grain Exchange Building next to the Federal Courthouse. They're in the phone book. Look them up."

Jack Ross needed a favor: "I have members who are desperate for work."

"There's not much that I can do to help you." Frank said. "I'm hoping for a shut-down for maintenance at the paper mill in Escanaba, but that will only last a few weeks. I don't know yet if any ironworkers will be needed. I'm waiting for a call."

"What about Quinnisec?"

"It will be winding down soon. and some of my own members are going to be laid off. What about the mall in Bloomington? Can you put anyone to work there?"

"I already have some of my ironworkers there, and I have a few working in Iowa and the Dakotas. It's the men who have been on strike at International Falls that need jobs. Boise-Cascade's mill expansion is not an option while there's a picket line. I heard that you chartered a bus to Saturday's rally. How many will be on it?"

"Who told you I chartered a bus? If anyone shows up from Michigan, they won't be on my bus because I didn't charter one."

"It's rumored that as many as fifty, mostly your ironworkers, will be coming from Quinnisec."

"Forget the rumors. It's your strike and I'm not involved."

"It's not my strike. It's a wildcat strike. You know that. Why do you think I was surprised when I saw the leaflet? But hey, the guys on the picket line appreciate the help."

Chapter Fourteen

Conrad Jorgensen was the son of a Minneapolis physician and the nurse who worked in his neighborhood clinic. She married her boss several months before Conrad's birth. An only child, he was their "Connie" until he met a girl named Constance. From that day forward, he insisted that he be addressed as Conrad. His parents obliged, but he continued to be "Connie" to many of his grade school classmates.

Conrad's parents thought of themselves as upper middle class and were proud of their ability to fund their son's college education. Doctor Jorgensen expected that the boy would be the successor to his practice. That Conrad chose to study law, rather than medicine, was both a surprise and a disappointment.

Conrad's law school experience exposed him to competing political influences. During his freshman year, he rejected the conservative views of his parents in favor of a more liberal ideology. During his senior year, while working as a part-time clerk for a large, corporate law firm, he joined the Republican Party. By the time he graduated and passed his bar examination, the name "Connie" had lost fashion and "Conrad" was his *Nom de Guerre*.

As an associate in the law firm for which he had clerked as a student, Conrad was tasked with helping small and medium-size businesses. He drafted personnel manuals, health and retirement plans and compliance documents mandated by regulatory agencies. When asked to assist in a large corporate client's effort to defeat a union organizing drive, he seized the opportunity. Soon, he was assisting other corporations in their legal battles with labor unions.

Jorgensen looked upon the labor movement as an existential threat to capitalism and free enterprise. When Harlan Dixon asked him to help BE&K respond to a wildcat strike, Conrad was quick to accept. That the strike was in International Falls also gave him an excuse to escape the confines of his office for a few days. He looked forward to visiting a part of Minnesota considered by city dwellers to be a haven for vacationers.

Dixon flew to Minneapolis from Birmingham. Mike Carr drove the three hundred miles south from International Falls. Both arrived at Jorgensen's office while the lawyer was speaking by telephone with

Seymour Hoekstra who called to say that he would not be attending in person but would be available by phone in his Virginia office if anyone wished to speak with him during the meeting. Jorgensen was dressed in a blue, pin-striped suit, white shirt and paisley necktie. His gray hair was neatly trimmed and he smelled faintly of cologne Bordering on corpulent, his belly strained against the buttons of his shirt and his jowls sagged a bit.

The office was carpeted in a pale green that matched the drapes framing a row of tall, narrow windows looking out onto 4th Street. The walls were decorated with framed diplomas, certificates of achievement and photographs of the lawyer in the company of prominent politicians, including a smiling Ronald Reagan in front of a large, American flag. Dixon recognized it as one of many such photographs for which Reagan posed during his presidency. Mike Carr was impressed.

The lawyer's mahogany desk in the center of the room was faux Empire on ball and claw feet. Jorgensen sat in a corner of the room, on one of two Chesterfield armchairs that faced a matching sofa on which he motioned for Dixon and Carr to sit. A secretary brought them a tray with a large Thermos, plastic cups and spoons and packets of sugar and powdered cream. She set the tray on a coffee table. While Dixon and Carr helped themselves, she took orders for a late lunch off a menu from a nearby delicatessen.

"How was your flight?" Jorgensen asked.

Dixon shrugged. "They pack you in like sardines," he said, "even in First Class. If they make airplanes any smaller there won't be room for a carry-on."

"The drive from the Falls was okay," Carr volunteered, "except for the last half hour. I'm not used to city freeways."

Mike Carr was a tall, slender forty-something with an angular face, dark eyes and straight, black hair. His engineering degree from Michigan Technological University was his passport to a career in an industry in which unions were a convenient source of skilled labor. He found the restrictions placed by BE&K on recruitment and hiring to be burdensome.

Jorgensen had a different view. "Unions weaponize seniority in order to force management to put up with incompetent workers."

He and Dixon shared a belief that unions play no useful role in an economy in which they invested no capital and took no entrepreneurial risk. Both men considered union membership to be a conflict of interest, arguing that workers should serve only one master. Dixon came to BE&K from a small company where, as a human resources director, he dealt with unions on a daily basis and considered them an impediment to sound management. He enjoyed the unfettered authority he wielded in the absence of unions at BE&K.

"BE&K is a merit shop," he boasted "Rank and pay are not entitlements. We reward skill and productivity and I can hire and fire without interference from outsiders."

"We are on the same page," Jorgensen agreed," and I'm looking forward to helping you put an end to the strike that you mentioned yesterday when we spoke on the phone."

"That's not what I have in mind," Dixon replied. "The strike is annoying, but the work is getting done and we've been able to keep to our schedule. We're not here because of the strike."

"If the strike's not the issue, what is?"

"We're here to talk about a so-called rally, a mass demonstration that's to take place on Saturday. Union members are being recruited from as far away as Michigan to show support for striking trade union members in International Falls. We anticipate a large turnout and we want to be prepared."

Jorgensen's secretary set a bag on the coffee table. In it were sandwiches wrapped in waxed paper, packets of mustard, ketchup and mayo and paper napkins. She left and returned with a pot of fresh coffee. While they ate, Jorgensen pressed Dixon for details.

"I recall reading about the strike some months ago," he said, "but there hasn't been any recent news in the Minneapolis papers. I don't remember what the strike is about, but the iron range has a history of labor strife. Is someone trying to organize your workers?"

"Not much chance of that," Dixon said. "Our southerners don't believe in unions. Right, Mike? You've been on the scene since the strike began."

"I'm not aware of any organizing effort by the men who are picketing," Car allowed, "but I'm a bit concerned about what might be happening inside."

"What do you mean, 'inside'?" Dixon asked. "What might be happening?

"Minnesota law requires a certain number of licensed electricians to be on site during construction. Our electricians aren't licensed here."

"Of course not," Dixon interrupted. "Get to the point."

"In order to be in compliance, I had to hire a few electricians with Minnesota licenses even though they belong to the electricians union."

Jorgensen cut in. "Are they attempting to organize your workforce?"

"I can't be certain," Carr answered, "but it's not unheard of for a union to salt a job."

Dixon wasn't familiar with the term and Mike had to explain.

"A salt is a union member sent to infiltrate a non-union shop in order to organize. It's possible that there is a salt among the licensed electricians I had to hire. I'm only saying that it's possible. I have no proof."

"Find out if there's a salt," Dixon demanded. "We know how to deal with union agitators. We'll come back to this when you know more. Show him the leaflet, Mike"

Carr handed the leaflet to Jorgensen and waited.

"There's certainly a potential for violence," the lawyer said after studying the leaflet and handing it back. "Outsiders don't have the inhibitions of home town protesters. Have there been problems on the picket line?"

"There has been some minor damage to vehicles," Mike acknowledged, "but nothing security hasn't been able to handle."

"You neglected to mention the incidents of vandalism that have been happening in the neighborhoods," Dixon added, "and they include at least one case of arson."

"There's certainly been vandalism in town," Mike agreed, "but the picket line has not been a problem, and the fire is still under investigation."

"If I am to persuade a court to issue an order prohibiting this rally," Jorgensen cut in, "I'll need to show why law enforcement would be unable to maintain order. If picketing has been peaceful, anonymous incidents in town are not likely to be enough to win the day."

"I don't expect you to get a court order in to stop the demonstration," Dixon said, "but if property is damaged or if anyone is injured during the event, I want the responsible party or parties held accountable."

"How many people do you have working on the project in International Falls?" Jorgensen asked.

"At the moment, we're in a brief lull," Mike replied. "Deliveries by our suppliers have been slowed by summer vacations and I've allowed some of our workers to take the week off because of the Labor Day holiday."

"How did Labor Day become an excuse for people to be off work for the entire week?" Dixon asked. "We have a production schedule to meet."

"Most of the men have a two or three day drive to return to their homes. Leaving the job after work on a Friday meant they would spend the weekend traveling. I gave them the rest of the week to visit families. The break will boost morale without impairing our ability to finish on schedule. I expect to have a full crew again by the Monday following the rally."

"How many will be there during the rally on Saturday?" Jorgensen asked.

"I'd estimate fewer than one hundred," Mike said.

"Why is this important?" Dixon asked.

"You want to evacuate the man camp before Saturday and get word to those who are already gone that they are not to return before Sunday," Jorgensen said.

"I don't understand," Dixon said. "What's the purpose?"

"If a mob of union protestors attacks your workforce, there will be injuries. If there are injuries, there will be claims—perhaps multiple claims—for compensation. BE&K has deep pockets. People will say that BE&K was warned and failed to protect them."

"The picketing has been at the construction gate," Dixon said. " What makes you think the rally will be at the man camp?"

"How many workers will be going through the construction gate on Saturday?" Jorgensen asked.

Dixon looked at Mike who was shaking his head. "Most will be in the man camp."

"Can you get them out of the man camp before Saturday?" Dixon asked.

"I'll see that it's done," Mike assured him.

"What about Alderton's guards?" Dixon asked" They don't work for us, but they are assigned by Boise-Cascade to provide security for BE&K property and personnel."

"If they're not BE&Ks employees, they're not BE&K's problem," Jorgensen said. "They will be witnesses to any acts of lawlessness that may occur."

But if they're attacked," Mike said, "they'll be outnumbered."

"Maybe we should ask for more guards," Dixon suggested. "BE&K can share the extra expense if it's only for the one day."

"Let the police earn their pay," Jorgensen replied. "Crowd control is in their job description."

"The local departments are small," Mike said. "They may not have enough officers to…"

"Don't argue with the lawyer," Dixon interrupted.

"If it will put you at ease," Jorgensen offered, "I can ask the governor to activate the National Guard."

"Do you think he would?" Dixon asked. "We don't know for sure what's going to happen on Saturday. Is this the right time to ask?"

Jorgensen smiled. "It's just a suggestion. The governor needs the support of organized labor. He's not likely to do something that would offend his base. I'm confident that the request won't be granted."

"Then why ask?"

"I'll issue a press release. It will give the Governor something to worry about. If the police can't maintain order and the governor doesn't send help, the public will want to know why. The press release will shift the focus away from BE&K."

Jorgensen made a number of other suggestions before the meeting ended. When Dixon and Carr returned to the outer office, Jorgensen's secretary handed each of them a small slip of paper.

"It's for the sandwiches," she explained. "You can pay me and I'll pay the deli on my way home. The coffee is Mister Jorgensen's treat."

Chapter Fifteen

"My crowd control experience begins and ends with high school football games," Chief Patterson lamented. "Even if my officers had proper training, I don't have a large enough force to manage a situation like the one we might be faced with on Saturday. I'm afraid I'll need all the help I can get."

"I can't offer you much," Sheriff Noonan replied. "My jail has to be staffed twenty-four seven. I may only be able to spare the few road patrol officers that were scheduled to be off-duty on Saturday, and I'll have to pay them overtime. There goes my budget."

"What about the State Patrol?" the Chief asked. "Do you think they might lend a hand?"

"We can let them know what we may be up against and ask if they can assign a few officers or have them on standby in case we need them."

"Will you make the call? You're familiar with their command structure."

"I'll make the call, but I wish we had a handle on how many are going to be at this rally."

"From the talk on the picket line, there'll be more than just a few Michigan ironworkers, and here's no telling where others might be coming from."

"The State Patrol will press me for number," the Sheriff said, "but there's really not much we will know until Saturday. I can only give them my guess."

" Guess big," the chief advised, " just to be on the safe side."

Frank LeClaire held a sheet of paper that the ironworker who was standing at his desk had handed him.

"How many of these were passed out at Quinnisec?"

"I can't say. Buck might know. I got this one from him."

"Why are you giving it to me?"

"I was in town for a doctor's appointment. I thought you might want me to bring some more to the job when I go back tomorrow."

Frank shook his head. "Thanks just the same, but everyone probably has one now."

When he was alone, Frank slipped the leaflet into a drawer. He picked up his phone and dialed Ernie Hunter in Escanaba. He got a busy signal, waited and dialed again. A female voice came on the line.

"Mister Hunter is in court this afternoon. I don't think he'll be back much before five. Can I have him call you?"

"Never mind."

He put the phone down, picked it up again and dialed Jack Ross in Duluth. Jack's secretary put him on hold and Frank listened to music while he waited.

"What's up?" Jack asked when the music stopped.

"Vivaldi."

"Huh? My secretary said you sounded upset."

"I am. I need to talk to you about about Saturday's rally at International Falls. Some of my ironworkers are going to be there. Will they be picketing or did you have something else in mind?'

"Whoa!" Jack cried. "Let's be clear. If there's a rally, it's got nothin' to do with me. I'm going to be right here in Duluth . Where are you going to be, Frank? Will you be coming to Minnesota with your members?"

"Hell no. But the leaflet makes it look like I'm sponsoring the event."

"I've seen the leaflet. Are you saying it's not authentic?"

"I'm saying that I did not give anyone permission to go public with it, which is now beside the point. Everyone who has seen it will think that I did it. That's why we have to call the rally off?"

"What do you mean by 'we'? Even if it ain't your leaflet, that doesn't make it mine."

"I got a bad feeling about this rally," Frank said. "There must be a way to call it off."

"I may have an idea."

"I'm listening. Jack."

"The Minnesota Building Trades Council is sponsoring its own rally on September 16. That's the Saturday after the one in International Falls. The Council's rally will take place at the state capitol in St. Paul. It's to be a protest against use of Minnesota taxpayer dollars to subsidize non-union construction.

"How does that help me?"

"Maybe you can get your members to forgo the September 9 rally and go to the one in Saint Paul instead."

"How am I gonna do that? They're already fired up about the rally at International Falls."

"Tell them that the St. Paul is more important. Tell them it will be much bigger than International Falls. There'll be politicians, celebrities, television news coverage. It will have national visibility."

"Even if I talk them into going to Saint Paul, that doesn't mean that they aren't going to show up at International Falls."

"It's was just an idea. Do you have a better one?"

Jack heard the dial tone and put down his phone in Duluth. In Marquette, Frank lifted his thumb, reached for his telephone directory and searched until he found the number he wanted. Five rings later, a voice came on the line.

" Northern Tours. Ted speaking. How can I help you?"

"What's it cost for a bus from Iron Mountain, Michigan, to St. Paul, Minnesota?"

"Depends. When do you need it?"

"Leaving Saturday, September 15, and returning the following day."

"How many will be going?"

"Don't know yet, but they'll be workers coming off a job in Quinnisec."

"Really? Those Quinnisec fellas sure like to travel. Did you say this time it's the Minnesota capitol?"

When Conrad Jorgensen entered the general aviation terminal at Falls International Airport, a Buick Electra sedan was parked nearby with its engine running and Tyrone Gate standing beside it. The lawyer decided not to keep the young pilot waiting at the airport. He gave him a two dollar tip before sending him back to Minneapolis. During the drive to a resort hotel off of Highway 71, south of the city, Tyrone sat next to an empty passenger seat. Jorgensen sat behind him, his face only partly visible until Tyrone adjusted the rear view mirror for a fuller view.

"How was your flight?" he asked when their eyes met.

"Fine," Jorgensen answered before he moved out of sight.

Tyrone carried Jorgensen's luggage and briefcase to a suite and was dismissed with instructions to return at eight o'clock the following morning. The lawyer hung his garment bag in a closet and unpacked his suitcase, putting his carefully folded underwear and socks into a dresser drawer. He opened his briefcase and removed several items including a schematic of the mill expansion project. A second schematic depicted the layout of the man camp. After studying them, side by side on on his king-size bed, he turned on the television and watched the news until it was time to order dinner.

On Thursday morning, Jorgensen and Tyrone toured the construction site. Afterward, Tyrone accompanied him to the man camp where the lawyer took photographs at multiple locations. He made notes on a yellow legal pad and highlighted the locations on the schematic drawings where he wanted surveillance cameras installed.

"The cameras are being air-freighted from Minneapolis," he told Tyrone. "They will be here later this afternoon and we'll set them up in the man camp. You and other guards will be responsible for protecting them."

"We've been stationed at the construction gate. What makes you think that Saturday's action will be at the man camp?"

"The demonstrators will assume that construction will be shut down on Saturday and that most of the work crew will be in the man camp. Boise-Cascade has agreed to let me use Alderton's security personnel to protect the equipment that will be installed inside the man camp. That's all you need to know."

Tyrone shrugged. "If the fence does't keep the protesters out, what then? Are we expected to eject them?"

"You will be stationed at the camera locations. If anyone gets inside, you are to protect the cameras."

Tyrone shrugged. Except for the pay, the job had been a disappointment. News of the rally lifted his spirits. Jorgensen seemed determined to spoil the party.

Chapter Sixteen

Hiram was among the first to leave the man camp on Friday. He took a window seat near the rear of the bus and slid a gym bag, stuffed with socks, underwear, a sweatsuit and an extra pair of jeans, onto an overhead rack. A week earlier, he had dismissed the idea of driving to Alabama in order to be with Betsy and the children. The fifteen hundred mile drive from International Falls to Dothan would leave too little time to visit before he would have to begin the return trip. It would have meant days and nights on the road with little or no sleep. There also was the expense to consider. His pickup truck was a gas guzzler and he would have to spend for meals at roadside diners or go without.

    He peered through the window and, when the bus began to move, he sat back. and closed his eyes. Not knowing where the bus was taking them, he felt as if he had been convicted and sentenced without a trial. He thought about asking , but it didn't matter.They were not going to Alabama. Of that much he was certain. He tried to sleep but couldn't. With his eyes closed, he imagined a landscape of trees and fields, and pastures with horses and cows. He listened to road sounds and the murmuring voices of the other passengers. When the bus came to a sudden, jarring stop, his eyes flew open and his dream vanished.

    Through the window, he saw men gathered around the bus. They were shaking their fists and yelling, but he couldn't understand their words over the noise of an idling engine and the shouts from men inside the bus. When an object, perhaps a brick, struck his window, Hiram flopped back in his seat. The window cracked, but did not shatter. The bus began to rock from side to side. A few passengers slid from their seats and stood in the aisle, but Hiram was hemmed in by a much heavier man sitting beside him. The man's hands gripped the seat in front of him, his eyes were opened wide and his face was frozen in a grimace.

    Sounds of approaching sirens were heard, the rocking ceased and the crowd noise outside began to fade. As the sirens grew louder, the crowd began to disperse and soon the sirens were the only sound that could be heard. Then there was silence, the bus doors opened, the driver stepped out into the street and two uniformed officers of the International Falls Police Department boarded.They made their way through the bus, scrutinizing the passengers, and stopping to ask questions. Satisfied that no one was injured, they left without a helpful description of any of the attackers. When the driver got back into his seat, the doors closed and the bus moved forward, continuing south on Highway 71.Hiram studied the large figure beside him. The man had not stirred and still stared straight ahead, but his grip had loosened and color was returning to his face. Hiram looked away, leaned back in his seat, closed his eyes and tried to remember his dream.

On Highway 53, at edge of the city, an old school bus, restored as a recreational camper, was detained by road patrol deputies of the Koochiching County Sheriff Department. They were responding to a radio dispatch reporting an attack on a bus transporting BE&K construction workers. The converted bus on Highway 53 had Illinois license plates that the deputies viewed as "suspicious." They escorted it to a nearby strip mall where they questioned the occupants who said they were union members from Chicago and had come to International Falls to take part in a rally protesting the use of scabs to build a paper mill.

"We went to the construction gate ," the driver explained. "We thought we'd find union members from all over the midwest but there was only a handful of pickets. They said we got here a day early. Can you believe it? The rally isn't until tomorrow."

The deputies were uncertain whether to believe it.

"Where were you going when we stopped you?"

"We were told there's a campground near here if we wanted to stay for the rally, but we decided to go home. We're more'n six hundred miles from Chicago and we already missed work yesterday and today. We gotta show up on Monday, or else."

They assured the deputies that they knew nothing about an attack on a bus carrying BE&K workers.

"We been on the road and we only made a couple stops for gas. We don't know about a bus with ….who'd you say was on it?"

The deputies patted them down and searched the bus for weapons. They found only beer and hard liquor. The driver insisted that he had not consumed any alcohol, but he conceded that some of the passengers might be "a wee bit under the weather."

"It's going to take us at least twelve hours to get back to Chicago. Can you tell us where we might get something to eat before my passengers enjoy too much more of the 'hair of the dog?'"

When the deputies were satisfied that the detainees were who they claimed to be, that none were the subject of an outstanding arrest warrant and that they had no apparent connection to the incident on Highway 71, they were allowed to continue on their way.

Several hundred miles east of International Falls, Buck Saari, Roger Beaudre and several other other union men shared pitchers of beer and thoughts about the rally.

"How many of us will be going?" Roger asked, "and what if the scabs have weapons?"

"Even if they don't have weapons," someone said, "the guards will be armed."

"The bus seats fifty," Buck said, " "It'll be waiting for us in the Industrial Park at 11:30 Central Time. I want fifty on board. Be there before midnight 'cause that's when it's gonna leave."

"What about that rally in St. Paul? Are we expected to be at that one too?"

Buck shrugged. "That's up to you. You can decide about Saint Paul later. This week we're going to International Falls. Bring something to eat and drink. We'll be on the road most of the night. Are you coming, Roger?"

Roger always had something extra in his lunch pail in case someone forgot.

When the phone rang, office hours were over and Ernie's secretary had left for the weekend. He rarely took phone calls after five-thirty and never on a Friday afternoon when he was looking forward to meeting Rachel for a fish fry at their favorite supper club. While she waited for him, she would order a table and sit at the bar with a glass of wine.

"Ernie Hunter here. Who's calling?" He hoped that someone had dialed a wrong number.

"I hate to bother you this close to the weekend, but I need some advice."

"Not a problem," Ernie sighed, looking at his watch. "What's up?"

"It's about the leaflet I showed you," Frank began "the one you said I should get rid of, and I thought I did, but it got out there and everyone has seen it and now …"

"Hold on. You lost me. What do you mean by you thought you got rid of it? Did you or didn't you? And who is the everyone who has seen it?"

"Someone must have got hold of it. Maybe it was Buck, but I can't say for sure. Whoever it was made copies. Just about everyone on the Quinnisec job has seen it. They're going to International Falls tomorrow."

"Are you going?"

"You told me not to."

"Right. So, what's the problem?"

"That's what I want you to tell me. Do I have a problem?"

"That depends on what happens tomorrow. If the rally is orderly there shouldn't be a problem."

"And if it ain't orderly?"

"That could be a problem. The leaflet has union fingerprints. You should disclaim it immediately and tell your members to stay home."

"They already left the job. I don't even know for sure who's going and who isn't. I tried to talk some of them into going to St. Paul instead. There's a rally there next week. But those I spoke to said they were going to the Falls regardless, and it's not just ironworkers. It's other trades, too."

"You need to distance yourself from the leaflet. Find Buck. If he's the one who's responsible for the leaflet, fire him."

"I can't fire him. He's elected to the executive board by the members. I can only replace him as chief steward. What good will that do now?."

"Then you better hope that nothing bad happens tomorrow. If it does, we'll worry about damage control."

"That's it?"

"That's it for now. I'm late for dinner. If I think of anything else, I'll call you."

Five minutes later, Ernie was waiting to order a drink. All the barstools were taken and Rachel, who was seated, offered him a sip of her wine. He kissed her on the cheek and reached for her glass.

"Thanks. Just a sip. I'm holding out for a martini."

The barmaid took his order. When the dining room hostess escorted a foursome from the bar, he grabbed an empty stool. By the time his martini arrived, it was almost six-thirty. By seven o'clock, the noise from the dining room was making conversation impossible.

"Let's finish our drinks and go someplace quiet," Rachel said in a voice barely audible over the noise from the dining room.

"It's Friday night," Ernie reminded her. "It'll be like this wherever we go except…."

He suggested a fast food restaurant where everything but the deep fried chicken was precooked, packaged and shipped for reheating in a microwave.

"Yuck!" She grimaced. "The original greasy spoon. Have you seen the kitchen? Yuck," she repeated.

"If that means you want a decent meal, we might as well wait here."

She sighed and set her empty wine glass on the bar. "At least when we get a table it will have cloth napkins and real silverware."

"The crowd will have thinned by then," he added, pointing to her empty glass. "Are you ready for another?"

By the time the hostess came for them, there were a few empty tables in the dining room. She led them to one near a window overlooking a garden in which several small, Japanese deer were grazing among the flowers and shrubs.

"I love watching them," Rachel exclaimed. "They're so delicate and calm, not like our nervous white tails. I can't imagine anyone wanting to shoot these little guys."

"Careful what you order," Ernie cautioned. "One or two of these little guys seem to have gone missing since the last time we were here."

"That's not funny," she growled. "By the way, why were you so late? You kept me sitting at the bar for almost an hour. I had to ward off several strange men who wanted to buy me drinks—lots of drinks."

"That's not funny either," he said. "I was on the phone with Frank LeClaire He's in a bit of a bind and was hoping I could help him out."

"And you did, of course."

"'Not this time. He'll have to figure this one out by himself."

"Can you tell me about it?"

"Not much to tell. At least, not yet. Hopefully not ever."

"So, tell me already."

"It's that wildcat strike at International Falls. There may be mass picketing tomorrow. It's being billed as a rally to support the strike, but it could turn into something more ominous."

"What's it got to do with Frank LeClaire?"

"He prepared a leaflet urging his members to take part. It was a bad idea and I told him so. That should have put an end to the matter."

"It didn't?"

Copies of the leaflet were handed out at the construction project in Quinnisec. That's where Frank's ironworkers, as well as other trades, have been working. Many will be going to the rally at International Falls."

"Are you upset that he didn't take your advice?"

"Frank says he thought the leaflet had been destroyed. Obviously, it wasn't. Someone made copies and distributed them. Frank says it wasn't him."

"Do you believe him?"

"It doesn't matter. If there's trouble tomorrow, Frank's union will own it whether he's telling the truth or not."

They set their menus down and looked up at the waitress standing at their table, order pad in hand. She smiled back at them:

"Can I get you another drink?"

Chapter Seventeen

Until his wife announced that she wanted a divorce, Frank didn't know that his marriage was in trouble. "You've lost the passion," she told him, "I see no reason to continue the relationship without it."

Frank thought she was talking about sex and asked if she had fallen for someone else.

"Would it matter?" She asked. "The union is your passion and marriage is not in your job description."

"My job depends on the support of my members. They vote for me because I'm dedicated to their cause."

"Well, you've lost my vote," she told him.

It was still daylight when Frank walked up Front Street toward Washington Avenue. A wind was coming off of Lake Superior, reminding him that summer was on its way out. Although he hadn't had dinner and was hungry, his thirst trumped his appetite and he opted for a beer at the Shamrock. The late afternoon crowd had dispersed and there were empty stools at the bar when Frank ordered a beer. He drank slowly and watched the bartender wash and rinse glasses in the sink behind the bar. Frank counted the glasses as they were slipped, stems up, onto an overhead rack.

"Sales of wine must be on the rise," he said.

The bartender didn't hear him over he jukebox.

Someone took the stool next to Frank. "What are you celebrating?" Ralph Koski was the business manager of the carpenters union.

"Bachelorhood, Ralph. I'm celebrating my bachelorhood. Let's drink to it together. I'll buy the first round 'cause you're still a married man. Where's your missus?"

"I took her shopping and dropped her off at home when she was done."

"No Friday night fish fry?"

"I offered, but she said she was tired. 'Okay by me,' I said, 'but I'm goin' over to the Shamrock.' I thought you'd be on your way to International Falls by now."

"Why would you think hat?"

"I saw the leaflet. You know the one. I thought about going, but Jack Ross said it's a wildcat strike. He says his union never authorized it. That's why I scrapped the idea. What made you decide to get involved?"

"I ain't involved. At least, I didn't intend to be. Someone else got hold of the leaflet and gave out copies. It wasn't me."

"If it wasn't you, who was it?"

"I have an idea who it might have been, but I have no proof. All I can say is it wasn't me."

Frank lifted his glass and drained it. The jukebox went silent. Ralph wondered if Frank was telling the truth. Frank wondered if Ralph believed him.

"Ready for another?" Ralph asked.

"Might's well."

When their glasses were empty again, Frank got off of his stool and stood. His legs felt steady. "I gotta go."

Ralph nodded. "Take care."

Outside, the streetlights were on. The wind stirred up a bit of dust along the curbing. Frank wondered how many union members would be going to the rally. They would be up most of the night, partying on the bus. He hadn't eaten, but he was tired and needed to sleep. He would have a big breakfast in the morning.

Conrad Jorgensen's dinner was delivered to his suite. The television was on but silent as it blinked mute images from scene to scene. When he finished eating, he turned the TV off and went to the lobby. Tyrone was waiting, sprawled on a lounge chair. Jorgensen had interrupted his poker game, one that began after a poolside meal of Chinese take away. Tyrone was about to increase his bets when the lawyer called, insisting that they return to the construction site and man camp for a final inspection. The call put an end to Tyrone's winning streak.

The moon was hidden behind clouds as they made a cursory examination of the cameras they had installed to capture images, front and rear, of anyone or anything passing through the construction gate. At the deserted man camp, trailer windows were dark, but there was light from the bulbs above each trailer door. The narrow beam of Tyrone's flashlight guided them around the yard as they retested the video equipment that they had installed and tested earlier in the day. Jorgensen tried to visualize men gathered at the construction gate. Then he imagined them outside of the man camp, pressing against the chain link fence, causing it to sway until Tyrone's voice distracted him.

"Do you really think they'll come here, to the man camp? It looks deserted."

"I had BE&K remove the workers, just in case."

Tyrone watched as Jorgensen rechecked the positioning of the cameras, making certain that they were focused where he wanted. Conversation between the two men was limited to Jorgensen asking Tyrone for tools and telling him where to aim his flashlight. The video cameras were on raised platforms and were aimed at the empty yard and unoccupied trailers. The guards would be on the platforms. They would be passive observers, like the cameras. Martial arts skills did not appear to Tyrone to be included in the lawyer's equation. When Jorgensen was satisfied with the camera settings, they left. Back at his motel, Tyrone's poolside poker game was over.

Ted Grissom drove his Northern Tours bus into the darkened warehouse parking lot half an hour before midnight. Several minutes later, he opened the door for Buck. Roger Beaudre climbed aboard and put a lunch pail and a small cooler in an overhead luggage rack before sitting with Buck, behind Grissom.

"Not a cloud in the sky," Roger said. "A great night for a bus ride."

"I see you brought refreshments," Buck observed. "Did you bring matches?"

"I don't smoke."

"Who said anything about smoking?"

"What?"

"Never mind."

Before Roger could ask again, Buck was greeting others. Some had bottles in brown paper bags. Some, like Roger, brought coolers. By the time Grissom drove the bus out of the parking lot shortly after midnight, fifty union members were aboard. Most were ironworkers, but there also were millwrights, pipe fitters, and members of several other trades They talked, laughed and drank until they grew tired and lapsed into silence. A few slept. Others tried but were unable. At eight-thirty in the morning, the bus came to a stop near the BE&K construction gate in International Falls. Passengers who were sleeping were wakened as Grissom opened he bus doors.

"Not here," Buck snapped. "There's been a slight change."

The doors closed and he gave Grissom directions that someone had scribbled on a piece of note paper. The bus moved forward. Minutes later, it joined a convoy of cars, pickup trucks, campers and other buses. Grissom pulled to a stop and the doors opened again. His passengers began to get out of their seats. Buck pushed Roger into the aisle and followed him down exit steps and out onto the pavement. Others were quick to join them and soon the bus was empty except for Grissom. Around the bus, men were getting out of other vehicles. Grissom watched the growing crowd move toward the fence that encircled the man camp.

In Marquette, Frank LeClaire drummed his fingers on his desk while waiting for Jack Ross to pick up the phone in Duluth. When he did, Frank asked, "What's happening in International Falls? I haven't been able to get any news on the television or the radio. The bus must be there by now, but I don't know what's going on. What are you hearing?"

"Do you really want to know?"

"Of course I want to know. Have you heard anything yet?"

"Yeah. I heard and it's bad."

"How bad?"

"The Governor was asked to send in the National Guard."

"Do you think he will?"

"I don't know. It's only been said on the news that he's putting them on standby."

"Any idea how many are taking part in the rally?"

"Depending on where you're getting your news, there could be anywhere from a few hundred to more than a thousand. I wouldn't exactly call it a rally. It sounds more like a riot."

"What makes you say that? Is there something else I should know?"

"The action is not at the construction site. It's at the man camp. The fence went down and they went in. One report has it that smoke is coming from some of the trailers."

"What are the police doing to get the situation under control?"

"I don't know. I haven't heard of any arrests yet, but there have been reports of minor injuries to one or more of the guards, I think. But there's some good news, too."

"What's that?"

"The scabs weren't in the man camp. They're gone. They were evacuated before the rally began."

"Where'd they go?"

"Your guess is as good as mine."

From his office at the construction site, Mike Carr heard the helicopter rotors. In a motel room several miles away, Jorgensen heard them too. He had sent a letter to the Governor and provided copies to local and statewide news media earlier in the week. According to published reports, the Governor was "keeping a close eye on the situation in International Falls." Sitting on the edge of the bed and listening to the rotors, the lawyer assumed that the National Guard had arrived. He was trying to think of more ways to put pressure on the Governor, when the telephone rang.

"I only know what I've heard on the radio," Mike Carr said. "There is nothing happening at the construction gate, but they're rioting at the man camp. I intend to stay where I am until it's over."

"When it's over," Jorgensen replied, "send someone to get me. I'll want to asses the damage."

Rachel put the phone down and called Ernie in from the back yard.

"It's Frank LeClaire," she shouted.

He shut off the power mower.

"What?"

"The phone," she repeated. "It's for you. Frank LeClaire."

"Tell him it's Saturday—my day off."

"You tell him. He's your client, not mine."

She rolled her eyes as Ernie brushed past.

"Yes, Frank. What is it?"

Frank repeated what Jack Ross told him."I have to know if you'll be available if I need you."

"It's Saturday and Escanaba is a long way from International Falls. I'll be in my office first thing Monday morning. What kind of help do you think you'll need?"

"How am I supposed to know? That's why I'm calling you."

"You sound worried. Take it easy.and tell me again. What's happening?"

When Ernie put the phone down, Rachel asked, "What was that about?"

"They're rioting at International Falls,"

He brushed past her again on his way outside to restart the power mower.

Chapter Eighteen

Sections of chain link fence were flattened and men surged over them on their way to the trailers. Some paused to overturn vehicles. A group surrounded a BE&K bus and rocked it until it fell over on its side. When they reached the trailers, they broke windows and forced doors open. Finding no scabs inside, they vented their rage on the contents, tossing furniture, bedding and clothing into the yard and setting them on fire.

    Hank Peterson was letting others rush past him until something hard slammed into him behind his right shoulder. He stumbled and would have gone down if someone hadn't grabbed him. When he turned to see who kept him from falling, he saw a security guard on the ground being kicked and stomped by heavy construction boots. One of the men near the guard wore a familiar jersey. Hank turned away and pressed forward against the flow of the mob rushing toward the trailers. He reached the downed fence and crossed it. Outside of the man camp, he stopped to catch his breath and tried to remember where he had parked.

    Inside the man camp, tear gas canisters were dropped from Minnesota State Patrol helicopters was causing panic. Men ran aimlessly, seeking to evade the noxious fumes. Buck's nostrils burned and his eyes watered, forcing him to join others in their attempt to escape. As they fled the man camp, most ran to their cars and pickup trucks. Others took the riot downtown where they smashed the windshields and headlamps of vehicles with southern plates. Several cars were overturned and set on fire and a few store windows were shattered.

    The sound of helicopter rotors was still audible when Buck climbed back into the Northern Tours bus. The doors closed, Ted Grissom goosed the idling engine and the bus rolled forward until, moments later, flashing lights and sirens brought it to an abrupt stop. The sirens went silent, the bus doors opened and Grissom got out. Uniformed deputies with drawn weapons got in. They ordered the passengers off the bus. Outside, they had them lean with raised hands pressed against the bus while they were patted down. City police officers arrived and identified several men that they had seen fleeing the man camp.

    Buck, Roger Beaudre and several others were placed under arrest. Buck's demand to be told what they were being charged with was met with silent stares. He, Roger and the others were handcuffed and shoved into the rear seats of patrol vehicles. The rest of Grissom's passengers were let back on the bus and allowed to leave.

Mike Carr was in his office, monitoring police radio transmissions, when he heard the sounds of police sirens, fire trucks and at least one ambulance. When helicopter rotors began beating overhead, he opened a window and peered skyward. The noise increased, warning him to remain indoors. He waited until the noise subsided and an uneasy calm was restored before venturing out. At the man camp, wisps of smoke lingered above the smoldering debris left in piles by firefighters. The remnant odor of tear gas permeated what remained of the camp. Mike expected to encounter a few security guards, but all were gone. After cordoning the area with yellow tape, the police left, too. Alone among the trailers, he inspected battered and overturned vehicles and a bus that lay on its side, like the carcass of a dead whale. He shuddered at the thought of what might have been had the man camp been occupied by the southerners who worked under his supervision. When he returned to his office, the telephone on his desk was ringing.

"I'm glad you're still at work," Conrad Jorgensen said. "I want you to gather up the cameras. They must be kept safe. Let's hope they weren't damaged."

"I just came from the man camp. The cameras appeared to be intact."

"We don't want anyone tampering with them."

"Everyone's gone."

"The police, too?"

"They left a while ago. There's no one in the camp."

"What about the guards?"

"They're gone, too. According to news reports, a few are being treated for minor injuries. One was taken to a hospital."

"The guards are supposed to be protecting the equipment. Where did they go?"

"They're probably having dinner somewhere. It's Saturday night. The rioters are gone. There's no one in the man camp. You have my word on it. We can go there in the morning."

Jorgensen thought it over and agreed to meet with Mike at daybreak. They would retrieve the cameras and deliver them to Jorgensen's lodging where they could view the images together. The lawyer's hope was that Mike would be able to identify some of the rioters.

"That's not likely," Mike told him. "Judging by the news media estimates of the numbers, many of them must have come from out of town. I might be able to recognize a few locals if they weren't wearing masks."

"The guards must be familiar with anyone who has been on the picket line," Jorgensen said. "They should be able to recognize them even if they had their faces covered."

"The guards may be your best witnesses," Mike agreed, " along with the police officers who were at the man camp."

"I need to meet with the Chief of Police and the Sheriff. I want to speak with every officer who was at the scene. I want them to view the video."

"The men in jail must know who caused the riot,' Mike offered. "They'll want leniency and may be willing to cooperate."

"We already know from the leaflet that the Michigan ironworkers are to blame," Jorgensen said. "I want to photograph the carnage close-up. We'll begin first thing tomorrow morning. Are you certain everyone is gone? We don't want anyone tampering with the evidence."

"I'm quite certain here's no one there, but I'll try to contact the guards. I'll tell them we need them for protection from looters."

"Ask about the guard that was taken to the hospital. Find out if his medical expenses are covered by insurance."

Officer Carmody stepped out of the shower and grabbed a towel. His wife watched him dry himself. In his robe and slippers, he followed her to the kitchen.

"Dinner can wait until you have time to unwind," she said. "Are you ready for a cold beer?"

The man camp was less than a mile from the Carmody home, and Molly Carmody spent much of the day listening to the radio. Fearing for her husband, she worried that a small force of police officers would be overwhelmed by the mob. Her anxiety peaked when she heard the beat of helicopter rotors above the house. Minutes later, it was reported on the news that the man camp was being teargassed.

"Whose copters were they?" she asked. "The radio said the Governor was asked to send the National Guard."

"The Guard was put on alert. The helicopters belonged to the State Patrol. They flew in low and dropped teargas canisters. That's what cleared everyone out."

"That put an end it?"

"That ended it inside the man camp, but rioters went downtown and did more damage, mostly to out-of-state vehicles. They broke a few store windows, too. Maybe they thought the owners were BE&K sympathizers."

He told her how the rioters pushed the fence down and stormed across it. "There must have been several hundred that went into the camp. There was no way we could have stopped them. They were too many."

"I saw smoke above the rooftops," she said. "It was drifting this way. When the helicopters flew over, I expected to hear guns going off."

"It was like a war zone, but as far as I know, there weren't any guns. We had our weapons, but we weren't being threatened. They were after the BE&K men in the trailers but the trailers were empty. I hate to imagine what would have happened if they had been occupied."

"Where were BE&K's men?"

"All I know is they were gone, but that didn't stop the mob from wrecking he place. They took out their anger on anything they could get their hands on. I think they even set a few trailers on fire."

"Were you able to recognize anyone?"

"I can't say that I saw any familiar faces. Many of them were wearing masks.They may or may not have been from here. There was a bus from Michigan. Some of its occupants were arrested on their way out of town."

"Were they at the man camp?"

"They were identified as having been there and were arrested and taken to jail. The rest on the bus were let go."

"Why were they let go? They should've been arrested, too. If they came from out of town, they were here to cause trouble."

"Not everyone went into the man camp. Some stayed outside the fence and watched. Those that went in with their faces covered couldn't be identified. Without a positive identification, we couldn't make an arrest. We did manage to intercept and arrest a few stragglers as they were leaving the camp."

"What are they being charged with?"

"They'll be charged with rioting, destruction of property and maybe arson. What they did went far beyond disturbing the peace. They even beat up a guard. I was told that he's in the hospital."

"You can add assault and battery to the list," she said. "How badly was he hurt?"

"Don't know yet."

"It doesn't matter," she said. "It's still assault and battery."

"I'll find out more on Monday when we meet with the county attorney. Much of what went on inside the man camp may have been caught on video. We'll get arrest warrants and criminal charges for everyone that we can identify."

"I kept the twins inside like you told me to. At first, they were upset. They wanted to ride their bikes to where all the noise was coming from, but I wouldn't let them. When the helicopters flew over, it frightened them and they quieted down."

"Where are they now?"

"I told them they couldn't go outside until you got home. They're in the back yard. I said they had to stay there. They can leave the yard after dinner if you think it's safe."

"It'll be safe, but let's tell them not to wander off. They should be in before dark. I'm not scheduled to work tomorrow. We can do something together, as a family."

Twin boys burst into the kitchen from the backyard.

"What's for supper?" they shouted.

At the Rainy Lake Medical Center, emergency room personnel tried to stop the internal hemorrhaging of a man who was brought in wearing an Alderton Security and Protection Corporation uniform. Law enforcement officers said they found him on the ground inside the BE&K man camp. He was still unconscious when the ambulance delivered him.

The medical team cut away his uniform and undergarments so that they could ready him for surgery to repair or remove a severely damaged spleen. He also appeared to have fractured ribs, a fractured jaw and possible left ankle and knee fractures. X-rays would be needed to obtain a full and accurate inventory of these and other possible injuries.

"This guy is built like a truck," a young doctor remarked. "Whoever did this to him must have been huge."

"It had to have been more than one that did it," a nurse observed, "and it probably wasn't just fists."

While she was covering the patient with a sheet and blanket, he stirred. A moan escaped his lips, but his eyes remained closed. She pulled up the side rails and they were ready to move him.

Chapter Nineteen

Ernie finished his gin martini and was ready to bite into the olive when the phone rang. He groaned and looked up from his living room recliner. A call at dinner time on a Saturday afternoon rarely brought good news. He waited for Rachel to answer on the kitchen extension. After the fifth ring, he set his glass down and lifted the receiver from the table next to him.

"Who's calling?"

"Have you been watching the news? They're calling it a riot."

"Who are 'they?"

"Jack Ross says it's been on all the Minnesota channels."

"Why are they calling it a riot?"

'They tore the fence down, stormed the man camp. They broke into the trailers and wrecked everything. They set stuff on fire. "

"Is it over?"

"Jack said he watched it from Duluth. It was on television."

"Yes, Frank. You told me. But is it over?"

'The police dropped tear gas from helicopters and everyone went crazy. They ran downtown and rioted some more."

"Where are you?"

"I'm at home in Marquette."

"What about Buck? Where is he?"

No answer.

"Where is Buck?"

"I don't know. He was going to be on the bus. Maybe he's on his way back."

"Then it's over?"

"As far as I know."

"Was anyone injured?"

"Not that I know of. Jack says that there weren't any scabs in the trailers. He says somebody must have tipped them off. Maybe they seen the leaflet."

"Was anyone arrested?"

"Yeah, but I don't know who or how many—just that they are in the Koochiching County Jail."

"How do you know that?"

"Jack told me. And I'm getting calls from wives, family members. They're in a panic."

"It's Saturday night. I'm about to have dinner. Why are you telling me all of this now?"

"Who else would I tell? If my members are in jail, they are going to need a lawyer, bail money, a way to get home. Where do I start?"

"You can start by calming down. You won't be getting anyone out of jail tonight and probably not until Monday. Do you know what anyone has been charged with?"

"Not really. Riot I suppose. Mayhem. Is that the right word? Maybe arson. There were fires. How can we find out who's in jail and why they're being held?"

"You're going to have to wait until formal charges are filed and a court is convened to arraign the defendants. That probably isn't going to happen until Monday at the earliest."

"My phone's been ringing off the hook. Give me something that I can say I got from a lawyer."

"You can say that panic won't help. You have to wait for the arraignments. That's when the charges will be read and bail will be set."

"Do you have any idea how much money will be needed for bail?"

"I haven't a clue; but anyone who is not a resident of Minnesota and has no local family or other community ties is likely to be consider a flight risk, in which event bail might be in a high amount."

"How high?" Frank asked. "Hundreds? Thousands?"

"I have no way of knowing. I'm not familiar with Minnesota's courts or its criminal justice system."

Ernie looked up. Rachel was standing in the doorway to the kitchen, hands on hips. He shrugged and spoke into the phone.

"Do you know how many got back on the bus to Michigan?"

"Not yet. There was supposed to be fifty when they left Iron Mountain. I have no idea how many went in their own vehicles. From what Jack heard on the news, there may be as many as a dozen men in jail. He doesn't know how many of them are from Michigan. I hope to know more when the bus arrives in Iron Mountain."

Ernie did not wait for Frank to ask him to be in court in Minnesota on Monday. It would mean he would have to spend most of Sunday on the road.

"They'll need a local attorney," he said, "someone who's familiar with the bail bondsmen, the prosecuting attorney and the judge. Ask your friend Jack for a recommendation."

"He said he would call me in the next half hour or so."

"Ask him to refer you to a lawyer in International Falls. Meanwhile, I'll see if there's anything on the late news. If you hear from Jack before midnight, you can call me back. Otherwise, don't call me until Monday morning after eight o'clock. I'll make it a point to be in my office by then."

When he put the phone down, Rachel was putting food on the table.

"Lamb and lentil stew." she said. "Remember? It's getting cold."

Ernie came to the table and she began ladling stew into a bowl, passing it to him before filling a bowl for herself. She passed a plate of bread and sat across from him.

"Butter's on the table. Help yourself."

"That was Frank LeClaire," he said even though she would know. "Some of his ironworkers were arrested during the rally at International Falls. The media is calling it a riot. Frank is pretty upset."

"Was anyone hurt?"

"He doesn't know."

"What does he expect you to do about it at dinnertime on a Saturday night?" She hesitated before adding, "Are you planning to practice law in Minnesota?"

"I'm not planning to do anything in Minnesota. I've never even been to International Falls. They say that winters there are the coldest in the nation—colder than the Upper Peninsula."

"That's pretty cold," she sighed, " and the stew's getting cold, too. There's more on the stove. I can reheat it if you want me to."

She watched him butter a slice of bread.

"I told him to call again when he has more information."

She let it pass, and they finished the meal in silence.

While the sun was slipping below the horizon, Jack Ross napped in his camper. When he wakened, he ate the bologna sandwich that Edith packed for him. He thirsted for something other than the tepid coffee in his Thermos. He also wanted someone to fill in the details of what happened at the man camp earlier in the day. It was dark out when he drove to Benny's Saloon.

The pool cues stood in their rack against the wall and the balls on the table were silent. The jukebox glowed but gave forth no sound. Shaken by the riot, the regulars that frequented Benny's most Saturday nights were playing it safe. Debbie glanced at her watch. But for the two seated at the bar, she would have closed early and gone home.

"I never expected to find you here tonight,"Jerome said. I would've thought you'd be as faraway as possible. I don't suppose you were at the man camp today."

The two had met on the picket line, which Jerome thought was odd because he had been told that Jack was not in favor of the strike.

"No, I wasn't at the man camp," Jack replied, " but I'm guessing you were there. Am I right?"

Jerome grinned. "I never seen anything like it. It was one helluva party."

"I heard that it got pretty rowdy," Jack said. "I can't say I'm sorry I missed it. When I got into town, I tried to get a look at the damage, but the place was cordoned off. Now that I'm here, I think I'll stick around for a while. Maybe I can get close enough to view the scene tomorrow."

"There ain't much to see," Jerome said, "just a lot of dented fenders, broken glass and some charred rubble. But stick around if you're curious. You got somewhere to stay the night?"

"I found a place to park my camper and take a nap. Now I'm wide awake. That's the trouble with naps."

"Hey Deb," Jerome called out. "Can you put something on the grill for my friend?"

Her hair was tied in a ponytail that fell to one side as she leaned an elbow on the bar.

"I got some burgers, but the grill ain't on. It'll take a few minutes to heat up."

"Don't bother," Jack said. " I ate what the wife put in my lunch pail, and she says I don't need any extra calories."

"How 'bout you?" Debbie asked hoping Jerome would pass too.

"Nah. I ain't hungry."

Jerome's glass was empty. "Can I buy you one?" Jack offered.

"Sure. Why not?"

"I forgot your name?"

"Jerome. Jerome Banks. And you're Jack Ross, right? We seen each other before—on the picket line. I'm pretty good with names."

"Listening to the car radio after I left Duluth, I heard that teargas forced the rioters to leave the man camp." Jack said. "But I missed the part about how the riot started."

"When the fence went down, all hell broke loose," Jerome began. "Everyone charged in— almost everyone. They were after the scabs. They were gonna thump the scabs. Know what I mean? But there weren't any scabs. They were gone."

"Gone where?"

"I don't know.There was only a few guards, and they stayed out of it—most of 'em, anyway."

Behind the bar, Debbie spit her gum into a paper napkin, folding it. She glanced at her watch again and said, "I thought the rally was going to be at the construction gate. Isn't that where everyone's been picketing.? How did they end up at the man camp?"

Jerome smelled a hint of spearmint when she spoke. "I don't exactly know," he said, "but that's where they went, so I followed."

"What about the guards?" Jack asked. "Where were they?"

"I didn't see any guards until after the fence went down. I'd say it went down easy"

"What's that supposed to mean?"

"Maybe it was meant to go down."

Debbie brought out a fresh stick of gum. "I thought you were going there to picket."

"No one was there to picket," Jerome replied. "That's for sure."

"How long did it last, this… uh….rally…or riot…whatever?" Jack asked.

"I didn't keep track of the time, but I'd say it was over pretty quick once the helicopters got there."

"Before that, where were the guards?" Jack asked. "Didn't they try to put a stop to what was happening?"

"The only guard I seen was down on the ground and they was putting the boots to him. Maybe he 'had it coming, but I don't really know. I didn't have anything to do with that part."

"What about the police?" Jack asked. "I heard that arrests were made."

Debbie shook her head. "You're lucky you ain't in jail, Jerome."

"I only watched. I didn't do anything to get arrested for."

"It was a riot," she said, "and you took part in it. Your wife's gonna have a fit if she hears."

"How's she gonna hear? You gonna tell her?"

A couple came in and sat at a table. Debbie sighed, but moved from behind the bar to take their order. The man was complaining about how the scabs were taking over the town. His wife was condemning the riot, blaming it on the strike and the unions. Debbie served their drinks and returned to the two men at the bar.

"Do either of you want another?"

"You ready for one?" Jack asked.

Jerome nodded. The couple at the table were still arguing. Debbie looked at her watch and wished it were closing time.

Chapter Twenty

Hank Peterson spent Saturday night nursing a bruised back and shoulder. He didn't think anything was broken, but he intended to see a doctor on Monday. His wife would insist on it even if he was feeling better. Until then, he would rely on the over-the-counter stuff she was using for her arthritis. He wished she had something to settle his nerves, too.

Mary was in bed, propped up by pillows stacked against the headboard. She sat with her legs tucked to one side. Hank sat on the edge of the bed while she massaged his back. The liniment made him wrinkle his nose.

"What did you hope to accomplish by going there?" she scolded. "When have you ever picketed at the man camp. Common sense should have told you there would be trouble."

She scooped more liniment from the jar and Hank winced even though she tried to apply it gently.

"I thought we were going to be at the construction gate," he said, "but when everyone went to the man camp, I wanted to see why. But you're right. I should have known better."

She rubbed a little harder, and he winced again.

"Not so hard," he complained. "When I got to the man camp, lots of others were already there— I'd guess hundreds in cars and pickup trucks. Some even came in buses. Many had their faces covered. I only recognized a few that were from town or that I been with on the picket line. The rest were strangers."

Mary's hands were small but the liniment warmed them as she rubbed, giving her arthritic fingers brief strength.

"Why else would strangers be there except to make trouble? You should have turned right around and come home."

"If I'd known it was going to turn out the way it did…"

"Nonsense. You went into the man camp with a bunch of trouble-makers. How foolish was that?"

I couldn't help it. When the fence went down, it was like a stampede. I was caught in it with everyone else. I tried to go back, but everyone was running and I couldn't get turned around. That's when this guard, a great big guy, he…"

Hank stopped to catch his breath. Mary rubbed more gently, wanting him to continue.

"The guard was coming at me and I tried to go around him. That's when it happened. Something hit me. It must have been him. I can't imagine who else."

"Why would he want to hit you. You say you were trying to get away?"

"I don't know why he hit me. I almost went down. He had no reason."

"You had no business being there. That was reason enough. And now you've got a nasty bruise. Why on earth…?"

She paused and scooped more liniment.

"I almost fell, but someone grabbed me. I didn't see who it was. When I looked back, the guard was on the ground, and I turned and went the other way."

She squeezed his shoulder, he groaned. She stopped rubbing and began wiping her hands on a towel.

"Do you know if the guard hit anyone else or was it just you?"

"I don't know. When I looked back, he was all curled up and they were kicking him."

"Didn't anyone try to stop them? Where were the police?"

"I didn't see any police in the man camp—just that one guard. But I heard sirens and I smelled smoke. Something must've been on fire and I wasn't gonna wait to see what it was."

"You old fool. You're lucky you're not in jail or worse. If it had been your head that got hit, you'd be in a hospital. You're gonna be black and blue come morning."

He didn't mind her scolding, and the icy heat felt good. He was even getting used to the smell, but he was feeling drowsy.

Get some sleep," she said. " I'll rub your back some more tomorrow."

It was almost midnight when Frank telephoned again. Ernie was in his easy chair watching a cable news channel. There had been nothing about the riot at International Falls, and Ernie expected Frank to have little to add to what he had said earlier."

"Jack says the bus is on its way back to Michigan, but he didn't know who or how many are on it. I'm going to Iron Mountain to meet it. I can fill you in when it arrives."

Ernie groaned. "It's late."

"Of course. What am I thinking. I don't even know what time I'll get back to Marquette. It's not the members on the bus that I'm worried about. They're the lucky ones. They ain't in jail."

"There's nothing you can do tonight for those that are in jail, which means there's no reason for you to call me before Monday."

"I know that, but I'll probably be up most of the night, unless I can catch some shuteye while I'm waiting for the bus."

Rachel came in from the bedroom and sat next to Ernie. The weather forecast was for clear skies and moderate temperatures. She picked up the TV remote and lowered the volume.

"Maybe I can meet with Jack tomorrow. I'll stop by at his home. If he's not in Duluth, he'll be in International Falls. Can you meet us at the courthouse Monday morning?"

"What good will that do? I'm not licensed to practice law in Minnesota and I represent the union, not its individual members. There could be conflicts of interest. Anyone who was arrested and is in jail will have to find someone else to represent them."

"What if I need legal advice, I mean, as the business manager of the union?"

Ernie sighed. "You can call me. I'm always available by telephone, but the best time would be Monday morning when I'm in the office."

"Right. Monday. Any other suggestions?"

"Nothing that comes to mind at the moment."

Ernie looked at Rachel who was yawning.

"By the way," Frank went on, "how much do lawyers charge to get people out of jail? Do they get paid by the hour, a flat fee or what? Do they have to have the money up front?"

"Depends on the lawyer."

"What about fines and court costs? Will I need executive board approval to help with those? I can call a special meeting."

"Let's take it a step at a time. Number one, you should not use union funds for your members' bail, legal fees, fines or costs. They were not arrested while conducting legitimate union business. Number two, I'd prefer to answer your questions on Monday."

Rachel turned the television off, gave Ernie a little wave and disappeared into the bedroom. Soon, she would be sleeping. He, too, was tired and wanted to finish the conversation. but Frank, however, wasn't finished.

"What about 'presumed innocent'? Aren't they presumed to be innocent until proven guilty?"

"Beyond a reasonable doubt," Ernie added, stifling a groan.

"Doesn't that mean I can help get them out of jail? Nobody's been convicted of anything yet. Can't I help them while they're still presumed to be innocent?"

"You represent the the union. You have a duty to protect it from liability."

"Liability? What liability?"

Ernie wished he hadn't brought it up.

"Someone might sue the union because of what some of its members did today."

"How can the union be held responsible for what members did ?"

"The leaflet can support an argument that the union sponsored a rally that became a riot. Using union funds for bail or to pay lawyers would only strengthen that argument. I am advising you to let your members fend for themselves. Keep the union out of it."

"What if I use my own money? Is there any law against that?"

Hesitant to slam the phone down, Ernie took a deep breath and paused. "Using your personal funds would be risky," he said. "The fact that you are a union officer muddies the water. But if the funds are your personal funds...."

"Then that's what I'll do. I'll use my own money."

"What makes you think you have enough?"

"I've got savings and I can borrow more if I need to."

"Before you do that, get the names of family members and friends who can help. They may not need your money. Let them put up their money first. That's not legal advice. It's just my suggestion."

"If that means you wont be billing me for it, thanks. I already have a list of names. I'll call you on Monday. Sorry I kept you up late."

Ernie eased out of his recliner. He couldn't remember who turned the television off. The kitchen lights were off too, but the bedroom lamp was still on. He undressed and got into his pajamas before fumbling with the switch and slipping beneath the covers.

"It's about time," Rachel whispered.

On Sunday morning, Chief Patterson and Sheriff Noonan reviewed the incident reports filed by their officers and deputies. The reports described the wreckage found both in and outside of the man camp. More than a dozen men had been arrested. Some were apprehended as they fled the tear gas. Others were taken off of the Michigan bus. A few were found wandering aimlessly in an unfamiliar town.

"The county attorney will want our recommendations," Noonan said, "and it makes no difference to me if someone's local or from out'a town. I'm for throwing the book at all of 'em—felony riot if we can't prove arson."

Patterson agreed. "Let's hope the cameras that lawyer installed will show who set the fires and who assaulted the guard. Whoever did these things may be in your jail. It'd be a shame if they left town."

"Even if they did leave," the sheriff added, "they can be extradited if we can identify them."

"The men that were taken off the bus have already been identified," Patterson said. "Maybe the officers who were at the scene can identify more rioters from the video."

The sheriff was reaching for his Stetson when the phone rang. He put the receiver to his ear and answered. A moment later he put the phone down and faced the Chief.

"The guard that was hospitalized is still in surgery. It's gonna be a while before they have an idea of what the outcome is likely to be. I can't think of any thing else we can do until tomorrow. We might as well go home."

Peterson followed Noonan out of the building. They paused on the sidewalk. An acrid odor, faint but unmistakable, still lingered.

"We need some wind to carry it away," the Chief said.

"Let's hope the stuff that's still smoldering doesn't reignite. Everyone has gone home. They won't be pleased if they get a Sunday call back."

Seymour Hoekstra liked to boast of Alderton Security's safety record. Although many of his guards had police or military training, he rarely gave them hazardous assignments. He only agreed to send men to International Falls after receiving assurances from Gunderson that the strike was peaceful. Boise-Cascade's mill manager assured Hoekstra that the men on the picket line were local citizens with whom he was familiar on a first-name basis.

"It's not even an official strike," Gunderson proclaimed. "It's just a handful of disgruntled construction workers putting on a show. They can be noisy, but they're not violent."

The assurances were seconded by Mike Carr, according to whom the picket line was "pretty dull stuff."

On Sunday morning, Hoekstra had several injured guards on his payroll. He called Gunderson to complain and lay blame.

"How was I to know ?" The mill manager asked, insisting that he had been misled by Carr. "He never told me that there was trouble brewing."

Hoekstra put the phone down, picked it up again and dialed Jorgensen.

"You knew what was coming," Hoekstra shouted. "You had BE&K get its men out of the man camp and you left my guards to face the mob alone."

"What could you have done if you had been warned?" Jorgensen countered. "You have a contract to provide security during a strike. You should have been prepared for something like this ."

"What happened on Saturday was no garden variety strike. I sent my people to International Falls to babysit a handful of docile pickets. I had no reason to prepare for a riot. But you saw it coming and you kept me in the dark. If you had warned me, I would have taken precautions."

"I took precautions," Jorgensen replied. "I asked the Governor to send the National Guard. He refused. Is that my fault? It's a good thing the State Patrol showed up. If it hadn't been for them...."

"The State Patrol flew over in helicopters. My guards were on the ground and were tear-gassed while being threatened and assaulted. My safety record is ruined."

Chapter Twenty-one

When Conrad Jorgensen dialed the number that Harlan Dixon had given him, BE&K's senior vice president was at home watching television and enjoying a Perfect Rob Roy. The Chicago Cubs had just won, 3 runs to 2, over the St. Lois Cardinals. Dixon put his drink aside and let the phone ring a half dozen times before he answered.

"Is this something that can wait until tomorrow?" he asked when Jorgensen identified himself. "I don't like doing business from home on the weekend."

"You said I should call you immediately with any new information about what happened at International Falls."

"Well then, let's have it."

"I just got off the phone with Alderton's man, Hoekstra. He says a couple of his security guards were injured today —mostly scrapes and bruises, but one man was hurt more seriously and was taken to a hospital."

"I thought the guards were told to keep a safe distance. You said they were only tasked with protecting the video equipment. Did the rioters go after the cameras, too?"

"Apparently one of the guards left his post and got into an altercation out in the yard. That was definitely counter to my instructions."

"Then we should be in the clear. Right?"

"Hoekstra says it's a black mark on his safety record. He's afraid that a workers' compensation claim will cause his premiums to increase. He blames BE&K."

"If his guard failed to follow your instructions, how is that BE&K's fault?"

"I'm not saying that there are grounds for a lawsuit. I'm not a personal injury lawyer. I just thought you'd want me to let you know."

"Thanks," Dixon growled. "Now I know." He hung up the phone and reached for his glass. The ice was melted, the seltzer was flat and the drink had a bitter taste.

In International Falls, Jorgensen dialed again. "Send up a fresh bottle of wine and charge it to my room."

At the Rainey Lake Medical Center, Tyrone's Sunday morning breakfast was the liquid flowing through a tube that descended from a plastic bag hung on a pole next to his bed. He turned his head so that he could watch the drip, drip, drip. When he lost count, his eyes followed the tube from the bag down to where it disappeared beneath the antiseptic freshness of clean, white bed linens. When he heard approaching footsteps, he tried to raise himself, but a stabbing pain in his chest forced him back. He could feel that beneath the sheets his right wrist was tethered to the bed rail, perhaps to prevent him from disturbing the needle in his arm. He closed his eyes and opened them again when something brushed against the foot of his bed, startling him.

"Good morning, Mister Gates," chirped a female voice. "How are we feeling today? Not the best, I would imagine. You've had a pretty rough go of it, but we're doing all we can to make you comfortable."

Tyrone was pleased that he was no longer alone. He tried to speak, but his jaw hurt and his lips were parched and swollen.

"Wa…ah…er." It was as if his voice belonged to someone else.

She lifted his head and his lips felt something cool and moist. He saw that she was blond, was wearing a white uniform and had a pleasant face.

"Mo….er"

She leaned over him and dabbed his mouth. A few more drops of moisture slipped between his lips before she disappeared. He had a moment of panic when the bed began to rise, tilting him slightly upright. Then she was there again and was holding a glass with a bent straw that she placed between his lips. She slipped a hand beneath his back and lifted him slightly forward so that he could draw and swallow until the pain returned, forcing him to ease against the pillows again.

"The doctor is just beginning his rounds," she said. "He'll be stopping in to see you in a little while. I'll come back when he gets here."

Tyrone tried to remember how he came to be in this place. It was a hospital. Of that he was certain. But where? He wanted a better view of his surroundings, but his pain kept him from sitting up. It was obvious that he wasn't going to be leaving anytime soon, and he closed his eyes. He dreamed of men in overalls, their voices uttering a garbled litany of curses and obscenities. A fence went down and they surged into the man camp.

Faces were hidden by masks. Those that were uncovered were contorted by anger.

When Tyrone left his guard post, he had no specific purpose in mind until he saw the man who made him think of a duck. The other guards sneered when he told them how he had frightened this duck who was coming toward him now, not quite running. When they were about to collide, Tyrone swung his flashlight, the long, heavy one that he could grip like a club. It landed with a dull thud across the duck's back, but he didn't go down. He should have gone down, but was still on his feet when someone—it could have been more than one— crashed into Tyrone from behind. His legs buckled and he went down. Men—he couldn't tell how many—stood over him and were kicking him. He wanted to get to his feet and fight them, but all he could do was curl his knees to his chest and cover his head with his arms and hands. They kicked him until the lights went out.

When Tyrone regained consciousness in a hospital bed, his left side ached and he felt pain across his chest. He didn't know how long he had been asleep or that it was Sunday. He didn't know that his jaw had been wired. He only knew that it didn't seem to be functioning. There was a tube in his nose and another that descended from a plastic bag hanging next to him. He wondered how long his awful dream was going to last.

The men taken from the Northern Tours bus, and others arrested were segregated from prisoners in the Koochiching county jail who were serving sentences for minor offenses or awaiting trial for serious crimes. All were exposed to the mix of odors coming from the kitchen, the latrines and the stale sweat of vagrants and drunks.

"We've given them something to think about," Buck said. "Next time we won't tip our hand."

"Forget about next time, someone grumbled. "I wanna know how long we're gonna be locked up this time."

"A few days in jail is no big deal, "Buck replied. "Worse things can happen in a strike. We took no casualties and we're getting free room and board."

"This ain't what I'd call a luxury vacation. I don't think they'll be serving steaks."

"If they do, I want mine medium rare," someone quipped.

"You can have steak after we get out," Buck said. "but first they have to bring us into court and set bail."

"Do we get to make phone calls? How are folks at home gonna know where we are?"

"Those that went back to Michigan on the bus know where we are," Buck assured him. "In the meantime, if anyone comes around asking questions, dummy up. We don't know anything."

"Don't they have to read us our rights and tell us that we don't have to answer any questions?" Roger was with Buck when the guard went down and when smoke began to pour from the one of trailers. "We have to stick together and say nothing about the guard."

"We saw nothing." Buck agreed.

Shortly after noon on Sunday, Frank pulled to the curb and parked in front of a modest, of-fifties ranch-style home. It had an attached garage and a white-shuttered picture window facing the street. He followed a narrow walk across a small lawn, took three steps up to a porch and knocked on the front door. Moments later, Jack Ross' wife, Edith, invited him in.

She was a short, plump, grey-haired woman who Frank guessed to be about the same age as her husband, or perhaps a bit younger. Her round face and soft complexion made it difficult to guess. She was wearing a blue housedress, and as he followed her to the kitchen, Frank couldn't help noticing her fuzzy, pink slippers. She was all smiles and remained standing after Frank was seated at a table next to a window that looked out upon a small back yard.

"If Jack's not home," Frank said, "I suppose he's gone to the Falls."

"He left yesterday in his camper. Can I pour you a cup? Brewed it first thing this morning and made a full pot," she said, lifting the pot from the stove. "It slipped my mind that Jack wasn't home. Cream or sugar?"

"Thanks. Black's fine. I knew he might not be here, but I'm going to the Falls too, and Duluth is on the way. I thought I might as well drop by, just in case."

She poured two cups of black coffee and sat across from him.

"I've already had my breakfast, but I can fix you something to eat if you'd like."

"The coffee's fine and I can't stay long. Besides, I need to lose a few pounds. I had some Trenary toast before I left Marquette."

She furrowed her brow.

"It's an Upper Peninsula treat," he explained. "Hard, dry toast sprinkled with sugar and cinnamon. We dip it in our coffee to soften it up. It's named for the town where it's made."

His stomach growled and she got up and went to a cupboard. When she returned, she had a package of oatmeal cookies that she opened, putting a few on a plate and setting it in front of him. When she sat again, he reached.

"Just one," he said. "I got on the road early. I guess I should have had a bigger breakfast."

"You sure I can't fix you something else— eggs, bacon?"

He shook his head.

"I know what went on at the Falls yesterday," she said. "Jack told me about it. You both knew what might happen, didn't you?"

Frank nodded. "We were hoping it wouldn't turn out the way it did. We never…"

He didn't finish the thought.

"Jack went to see what he can do for his ironworkers," she said, "the ones that are in jail. That's why you're on your way there, too, isn't it— to help get your members out of jail? Jack calls it 'damage control.'"

"I intend to be in court tomorrow morning. Like you said, or as Jack said, to try to control the damage."

"I imagine they'll need money for bail and a lawyer. What else?"

"They'll all need transportation to get back to Michigan. I've been on the phone with wives and mothers. Most of them aren't able to be in court tomorrow, although one or two said they'd try. That leaves me to help get them out and get them home."

"Well, a man can't work on an empty stomach," she said. "You better let me fix you something to eat before you go."

Although it was almost one o'clock and he wanted to be on his way, Frank accepted the offer and watched as she warmed some leftover meatloaf and mashed potatoes. She put together a salad, set out bread and butter and poured a tall glass of milk. Then she sat and watched while he ate. When he finished, she cleared the table, poured more coffee and helped him to a slice of rhubarb pie. When he wedged himself behind the wheel and put the key in the ignition, it was two-thirty in the afternoon. Three hours later, he reached International Falls and checked into a motel. His stomach was full and he was ready for a nap.

Chapter Twenty-two

Northern Minnesota's forests, much like those of Michigan's Upper Peninsula, display various shades of green during spring and summer. In the fall, deciduous trees burst into brilliant hues of yellow, orange and red. Between Duluth and International Falls, there were enough hints of fall to remind Frank that deer hunting season was not far off, and he made a mental note to let his beard grow for the occasion. His thoughts were interrupted when an antler-less whitetail leaped onto the highway, forcing him to slam in his brakes and squeal to a stop. The large doe passed in front of him and, when it disappeared, he waited to allow a second deer and a third, both smaller than the first, to saunter across. Such stupid animals, he thought as he eased his foot off the brake pedal and moved forward.

It was still daylight when he checked into a motel. He tossed his gym bag on a bed and threw himself on the other. Within minutes, he was snoring. When he awoke, it was dark. Jack's wife knew what she was talking about when she suggested that Frank look for her husband at Benny's Saloon. When he got there, Jack was sitting alone at a table, eating a cudighi and nursing a tall glass of beer. Frank pulled back a chair and sat. Neither man spoke until Jack finished eating and broke the silence.

"Edith told me you were on your way here. You left a few minutes before I phoned her. She said she told you where to look for me."

"She also fed me. How come you ain't fat?"

Jack grinned. Debbie came to take Frank's order.

"What'll it be?"

"Nothing to eat," Frank said, "but I'll have one of those. He pointed to Jack's empty mug. "And bring him another too."

Jack nodded and they watched her return to the bar, admiring the sway of her hips and the way her slacks hugged her behind. Frank wondered what she would be like in bed.

"Are you thinking of making a pass at her," Jack asked. "or would you like me to tell you what happened at the man camp yesterday?"

"The radio news on my way here made it sound pretty bad. I know you weren't there, but how bad was it?"

"The man camp was demolished—most of it—cars, trucks, trailers— some beyond repair."

"Was anyone hurt?"

"A couple of security guards got hit with flying objects. One left in an ambulance. I haven't heard what happened to him."

"How did it end?"

"The State Patrol 'copters dropped their canisters in the man camp, and the teargas spoiled the party. But they took it downtown and celebrated some more."

"How many were arrested?"

"Don't know, yet. The news didn't give any details except that some were your guys and some were mine. There may have been others, too, but I don't know that for a fact."

"Have you been to the man camp to look at the damage?"

"I went there, but it was cordoned off. I didn't want to get too close and be mistaken for a rioter returning to the scene."

"Maybe we both can get a look at it tomorrow."

"We can try. I already have a pretty good idea of what we'll see. Now that you're here, what can I do to help you?"

"I want to get my members get out of jail. They'll need a bail bondsman and a good lawyer. Got any suggestions?"

"Already have it covered. The bondsman has been alerted and I lined up a lawyer—a youngster who's fairly new but eager. He said he'd show up for the arraignments and try to get bail set as low as possible. He intends to have everyone plead 'not guilty.' That'll give him time to sort things out. He's worried about your guys."

"Why is that?"

"Flight risk. It's because they're not from here."

"Their folks back home will put up some of the money and I'll put up the rest. No one will jump bail."

"The court might not be as confident as you are. The lawyer also wants to know who's gonna pay his bill for your guys."

"I'll see that he gets paid for what he does tomorrow. Is he willing to take the cases further? How much will that cost?"

"He said it's too soon to know."

"That's what they all say. What else did he tell you?"

"He says he doesn't know if he'll be able to represent everyone. There might be conflicts of interest. He needs to know who's being charged with what and what deals, if any, the prosecution is willing to offer. He says some of our people might be asked to testify against others."

"Why am I getting the impression your lawyer has more questions than answers. Does he have any experience with this sort of thing?"

"I doubt that anyone around here does. This is my first riot—yours too, I bet. Maybe we should think about getting a lawyer from Duluth or the cities. I can make some inquiries if you want me to."

"I have a lawyer in Escanaba who does our union's work. I don't know if he'd be willing to get involved, but I can ask."

"Tomorrow we'll know what the charges are. Who will be putting up bail for your members and how is the money getting here?" Jack asked.

"I'm going to have my bank wire the money."

"From what account? You're not thinking of using union funds are you?"

"You don't have to tell me. I've already been schooled. I'm going to put up my own money. I don't expect any family or friends from Michigan to show up in the morning. That's why I'm here. What are you going to do for your members?"

"I'm only a spectator. My members have family and friends in Minnesota. I'm here to offer moral support. Where are you staying? My camper is parked a mile or two from here. I've got plenty of room."

"Thanks, but I'm all set. Let's meet at my motel in the morning. You can leave your camper there and we'll take my car and have breakfast somewhere close to the courthouse."

Debbie returned with fresh glasses, set them on the table and picked up the empties.

"One tab or two?" she asked.

Frank looked at her. She smiled. He smiled back and reached for his wallet, but Jack waved him off.

"I started a tab before you got here. These are on me."

"My turn next time," Frank said, and his eyes followed Debbie to the bar.

While Conrad Jorgensen waited for room service to deliver his dinner, he watched one of the videos retrieved from the man camp by Mike Carr. Of particular interest was the image of a uniformed guard being knocked to the ground, kicked and beaten by rioters. The tallest of the assailants appeared to be wearing an athletic team jersey, but his image was partially obscured by others gathered around the fallen guard. Jorgensen was about to rewind and view the scene again when there was a knock and a voice from the hall.

"Room service."

A tray was set on a table in the sitting lounge of his suite. He signed for the meal adding a ten per cent tip, a bit of extravagance he would include when he submitted his travel expense voucher. When he was alone again, he lifted the lid and uncovered a ten ounce filet, medium rare, with mushrooms, Brussels sprouts, twice-baked potato and a side salad with raspberry vinaigrette. He would have preferred to begin with half a dozen raw oysters, but it was Sunday and he worried that they might not be fresh. A bottle of Cabernet, a wine glass and a corkscrew sat next to the tray. Jorgensen frowned. The bottle was unopened. Regretting the tip, he picked up the corkscrew.

When he was finished with his meal, he set the half-empty wine bottle on the nightstand next to his bed and slid the tray into the hallway. He would finish the wine before going to sleep and would be up early to shave, shower and dress for court. He intended to meet with Carr and Gunderson to see if they could identify any of the rioters caught on film.

Hiram Pardee stuffed paper plates, plastic utensils and empty quart containers into the large, paper bag in which they were delivered to the motel. He dropped the bag into a trash barrel in a corner of the conference room where he and several other BE&K workers had shared an evening meal of Chinese take away, before adjourning to the lobby and settling onto vinyl upholstered sofas and chairs. They guessed that they were somewhere in the vicinity of Duluth.

"How long do you figure we'll be here?" someone asked.

No one answered because no one knew.

"Are you in a hurry?" asked someone else. "This is like a vacation, and it's a helluva lot safer and more comfortable than the trailers. We even have a swimming pool. Did anyone bring a swimsuit? If not, we can go skinny dipping."

On Saturday, they had listened to radio reports of the riot. There was television coverage later that evening. Most of the Sunday night news reports were a repeat of what had been broadcast the day before. The man camp had been under siege and Hiram worried that his pickup truck was among the vehicles that were vandalized. Someone began shuffling a deck of cards.

"How 'bout some nickel-dime poker, pot limit. Cut for the deal."

"What's the ante?"

Hiram left the lobby and returned to the room that he shared with two others. While they played, he would think about Betsy and the children and how happy they would be when they were reunited.

Tyrone was awake when the nurse came to check his vitals. The door to his room was partly open and she pulled a curtain around his bed, shielding him from the light from the hallway. There had been a shift change. She was different, smaller than the other one. It was difficult to make out her features. Maybe it was the softness of her step that made him think that she also was younger. He assumed that it was newer employees who would be assigned to the the night shift.

She wrapped his arm in a sleeve and he felt the compression build to a peak before it expired with a rush. He wanted her to tell him that his blood pressure was normal, but she said nothing. Then, she was doing something with his other arm, the one that was tethered to the bedrail. Afterward, she hung a new bag on the post beside his bed. Tyrone listened to the steady beep-beep-beep coming from a monitor behind him. He remembered that he was thirsty again and he hoped she would give him some water. But she didn't hear what he was thinking and he fell asleep.

At five minutes after eight on Monday morning, Chief Patterson and Sheriff Noonan were in the office of the county attorney. Arnold Webster, a small man in his late fifties, was bespectacled and kept his straight, thinning hair combed over his emerging baldness. A former criminal defense lawyer and third term prosecutor, Webster was well versed in Minnesota criminal law and procedure, but like Patterson and Noonan, he had never dealt with the aftermath of a riot.

Webster was sympathetic to the cause of the wildcat strikers. Most were local people whom he looked upon as constituents. He was angered, however, by the intrusion of their Michigan allies. He considered them "outside agitators" and he was certain that they were responsible for Saturday's riot as well as some of the recent vandalism.

"If there had been any fatalities, I'd be charging every one of them with first degree riot and have them sent to prison for twenty years," he declared.

"The guard is alive, but not out of the woods yet," the Sheriff said. "His condition is still listed as critical, but he's expected to survive."

"If there's evidence that a weapon was used," Webster added, "Ill charge second degree riot with carries a penalty of up to five years in prison."

"We saw no mention of weapons in any of the reports," Patterson said, "but we could have missed something."

Noonan shook his head. "My deputies searched the bus and everyone that was on it. They found nothing that looked like it could have been used as a weapon."

"Nothing was found on those that were arrested as they were leaving the man camp," Patterson added. "If they did have weapons, they got rid of them before they came out. There were things inside the camp that could have been used as weapons—hammers, spud wrenches, metal pipes. But no one was found in actual possession."

"Even if no weapons were found, I can charge third degree riot and ask for a year in jail and a stiff fine. That's what I intend to charge at the arraignments this morning. We can keep the more serious charges on hold until we see that lawyer's videos. Let's hope they shed some light on who attacked the guard and who set the fires."

"What about conspiracy?" Patterson asked. "Wouldn't that carry a stiffer penalty?"

"Under federal law, yes, but not in Minnesota law," Webster explained.

"Maybe you should bring the feds in on this."

"I didn't approve of Boise-Cascade's decision to hire southerners to do work that our local people could do, and I'm not going to ask the feds to do my job. I'll charge each defendant with third degree riot, which we should have no difficulty proving."

"But we know that there was arson," Patterson persisted, "and we have a guard who was badly injured, possibly with a weapon. Whoever did these things deserves more than a year in jail."

"I want to see what we have on video," Webster repeated, "and let's hope the guard has a good recovery."

"He was conscious when I checked on him earlier this morning," Noonan offered, "but I was told that he's still in a lot of pain. They don't think he'll die, but he's going to have some long term problems. They don't know if he'll be able to walk again."

"Keep checking on him," Webster said. "I want to stay informed, especially if his condition worsens."

Tyrone could have told them a great deal about his condition if he were able to talk. In order to repair his facial bone fractures, cuts were made lengthwise along his jaw so that it could be re-positioned. Screws were used to hold bone together while his chin was moved forward and secured with plates and more screws. As a result, his face was swollen beyond recognition. Add the pain of a partial splenectomy, multiple rib fractures, a crushed ankle, shattered kneecap and a neck sprain, and there could be no doubt that the former high school football hero and martial arts expert was having a very bad day. The doctor did not have to tell him that it would be a while before he would walk, talk or chew a piece of meat. The assurance that he was not going to die seemed a questionable blessing.

Chapter Twenty-three

Wanda took breakfast orders when she wasn't bringing trays from the kitchen. When she stopped to fish a check from her apron pocket, Jack reached for his wallet, but was too late. Frank handed Wanda several bills.

"Keep it."

"Thanks," she grinned, "Have a nice day."

Outside, it was sunny, but the air was cool with a light wind. Jack wore jeans, a white shirt and a blue blazer. Frank was dressed in tan slacks and a sweater under a worsted sport coat. Neither man had a tie or hat as they walked several blocks to the courthouse on 4th Street, leaving Frank's Crown Victoria parked near Lulu's.

The Koochiching County courthouse is a Classical Revival, brick building with a stately dome. It was completed in 1909 and was added to the National Register of Historic Places in 1977. Within its walls, the district court presides over family, probate and juvenile matters, civil lawsuits, and criminal and traffic offenses. On Monday, September 11, 1989, multiple defendants who had been arrested two days earlier were to be arraigned. When Frank and Jack entered the courtroom, a young lawyer was standing at a table in front of the judge's unoccupied bench. Jack introduced Frank to Mark Murphy. Yet to arrive were Webster, Noonan and Patterson .

"Jack says that you'll go good for my fee," Murphy said. "Is that right?"

"I don't know what you intend to charge, but Jack says I can trust you. That's good enough for me. Tell me how much and I'll see that you get paid."

Murphy wrote a dollar figure on his legal pad and showed it to Frank, who nodded. They shook hands and took no notice of the middle-aged man in a dark blue suit and vest who stepped quietly into the courtroom and took a seat in the rear of the gallery. Reluctant to draw attention to himself by moving closer, he was unable to hear the conversation at the table, but assumed that it was about the pending arraignments. He remained seated while more spectators, including a reporter from the local newspaper, filed in.

Frank and Jack took seats in the first row of the gallery. Webster entered the courtroom through a side door and led Patterson and Noonan to the table next to Murphy. When the bailiff called the room to order, all stood and remained quiet while the judge made his entrance and took his place on the bench. Moments later, uniformed deputies escorted their prisoners into the courtroom. Having had little sleep during their two nights in jail, they were unshaven and unkempt. They stood before the bench and waited while the black-robed figure sitting above them shuffled through a stack of papers. Satisfied that each complaint contained the proper, redundant language, he read the charge aloud.

"Each of you is accused of having committed the offense of third degree riot."

He told them of the maximum penalty that could be imposed if convicted, and he sighed as if it were a gift, adding: "Whether the prosecutor will be adding more serious charges remains to be seen."

After advising them of their rights, the judge asked each defendant for a plea and each replied, "not guilty," as Murphy had instructed them to do. The proceedings were formal, brief and seemingly inconsequential until the question of bail was reached. The judge shuffled through the stack of complaints one more time.

"A number of you have given a Michigan address as your place of residence. Does anyone from Michigan who is presently before me own real estate in Minnesota?"

Silence.

"Does anyone who is here from Michigan have immediate family or a close relative living in Minnesota?"

Again, silence.

From the rear of the courtroom, Conrad Jorgensen stared at a familiar jersey. On Sunday, the Green Bay Packers lost to the Tampa Bay Buccaneers. That night, Jorgensen watched television news clips of some of the game's key plays. "Majkowski" was the name emblazoned over the number 7 on the quarterback's jersey. In one of the the videos of the riot, the name and number on the back of a team jersey wasn't visible, but the colors were unmistakable. The Magic Man and his team may have disappointed yesterday's Packer fans, but the tall man standing before the judge appeared to be someone Jorgensen and the police were hoping to find. With his back to the gallery, the profile seen on Jorgensen's video was not in view. But Jorgensen was certain that Buck was one of the men standing over the fallen guard.

When the arraignments were over, the prisoners were escorted from the courtroom and returned to the jail where they would remain until bail was posted. For each of the defendants from Michigan, bail was set at fifty thousand dollars. A bondsman posting that amount would charge ten per cent, to be paid up front. Frank was disappointed, but not surprised.

"If anyone is unable come up with the entire amount for the bondsman," he told Murphy, "I'll make up the difference."

Frank, Jack and Murphy left the building, but Jorgensen stayed behind and waited in the hallway outside the courtroom. When Webster emerged, Jorgensen intercepted him.

"We have to talk," he declared. "I have information concerning one of the men who was arraigned—the one wearing the Green Bay Packer jersey."

"My office is down the hall," Webster replied. "We can talk there."

He led the way with Jorgensen at his side and Noonan and Patterson close behind. When they reached his office, Webster asked them to be seated while he took his place behind an ancient desk strewn with file folders, typed documents and legal pads with handwritten notes. After removing a ballpoint pen from a drawer, he selected a pad, flipped to a blank page and waited for Jorgensen to begin.

In Mark Murphy's office a few blocks from the courthouse, Frank and Jack listened while the young lawyer told them what to expect by way of further proceedings. Frank was eager to return to Marquette.

"It's almost noon here. That means that it's close to one o'clock in Michigan. Unless you need me to stay, I can be home before dark and be able to do my banking first thing in the morning ."

"I see no reason to keep either of you," Murphy replied.

"I intend to remain in town tonight," Jack said. "I told Edith not to wait up for me. I want to meet my members when they're released from jail."

"My members will need transportation to return to Michigan," Frank told them. "I'll charter a bus, but it won't get here until Wednesday.

If they are released from jail tomorrow, they'll need a place to spend the night."

"I can help," Jack offered. "I'll reserve motel rooms and put it on my credit card. You can reimburse me later."

"You might as well add pizza and beer to your card," Frank suggested. "I'm sure they've had their fill of jail food by now."

In a corner of a crowded jail cell, Roger Beaudre's head throbbed, his body ached and he was shivering as he wrapped his arms around himself. The jail's odors were making him nauseous and he tried not to think about the food.

"I think I'm coming down with the flu," he moaned. "I need to lay down."

Several men stood and offered a bench to him before moving away. Roger eased himself down, still shivering.

Buck removed his jersey and handed it to Roger.

"Put this on."

Roger pulled Buck's jersey over his head and slipped his arms through sleeves that were too long and had to be rolled back

"Thanks," he said. "This will help."

Buck moved away and Roger curled his knees up to his chest and closed his eyes. He was dozing when a deputy rattled the bars of the cell with his jail keys.

"Whoever's wearing a Green Bay Packer jersey better get over here."

Someone nudged Roger, then shook him. He struggled to his feet and waited for someone to tell him why his sleep was being disturbed when his head still ached. The deputy repeated himself and Roger was pushed forward. Buck eased himself toward the rear of the cell.

"Move it," the deputy growled. "I ain't got all day."

"Why me'?" Roger asked when he reached the cell door. "I ain't done nothin."

"Yeah. Why him?" someone repeated. "He ain't done nothin."

"Because I'm a Viking fan," the deputy answered. "So get his Packer butt over here."

He opened the cell door, closing and locking it as soon as Roger was in the hallway. The men in the cell listened to receding footsteps until they heard a metal door slam shut. Then there as silence.

When Roger and the deputy reached the county attorney's office, Webster, Jorgensen, Noonan and Patterson were waiting. Moments later, they were joined by Mark Murphy.

"I thought we'd better have the lawyer present," Webster explained. "If we get a positive identification, we don't want anyone complaining that we didn't do it by the book."

Webster aimed a remote at a small television screen. He backed up a video to the beginning of a segment that they had previewed while waiting for Roger to be brought over from the jail. When Webster hit the stop button, they were looking at an image of several men standing over someone on the ground, wearing what appeared to be a uniform. The tallest of the men standing over him, seen in profile, wore a green and gold jersey with white hashmarks on the sleeve. The number on the back, if there was one, was not visible.

When Webster hit the "play" button, booted feet could be seen kicking the man on the ground. Whether any of the boots belonged to the man in the green and gold Jersey was unclear, but the jersey looked to be a snug fit on a heavy-set frame. The jersey Roger Beaudre had on hung well below his waist and the rolled sleeves were too long.

"Where did you get that jersey?" Jorgensen demanded, pushing himself between Roger and Mark Murphy. Roger's mouth opened as if he were about to speak, but Murphy cut in. "This is not going to be an interrogation. I'm instructing him to remain silent and not answer any questions."

Jorgensen looked to Webster for help.

"You have had your view, Mister Jorgensen. That's all I can give you. I can't make him answer any questions."

"But what about the jersey," Jorgensen stammered. "It doesn't fit him. It's made for a much larger man. We need to know where he got it."

"I can see what concerns you, but I'm afraid I can't help you. He's got rights. Unless there's something else we can accomplish while he's here, the deputy can return Mister Beaudre to the lockup."

When Roger was in the jail cell again, Buck pointed to the Packer jersey.

"Did anyone ask you about it?"

"I think you better let me wear it a while longer," Roger suggested, "at least until we get back to Michigan."

Frank LeClaire wired the proceeds of his bank loan to Mark Murphy's trust account in International Falls. Murphy paid the bondsman and bail was posted for the jailed, Michigan defendants. Jack Ross chauffeured them to Benny's Saloon where, with some help from Jack, they pooled enough money for burgers and pitchers of beer. Jack left to reserve motel rooms, leaving Roger in one after promising to bring him some soup from Lulu's Cafe.

Chapter Twenty-four

Jerome thirsted for a shot of bourbon. A double would be even better. His wife was at her mother's and was refusing to take his phone calls. The possibility that she might be gone for good had him vacillating between panic and relief. Also weighing on him was his guilty plea and the sentence he was serving for being a disorderly person. He had agreed to admit guilt and pay to replace the broken windows under threat of having to answer to the more serious charge of malicious destruction. Ordered to abstain from alcohol during six months of probation, he was having second thoughts about his plea.

Jerome blamed his troubles on Boise-Cascade. If the mill expansion had been given to a union contractor, he would be working, his wife would be home and he might not need to drink. But he had no job, his wife was AWOL and his thirst was real. When he pulled open the door to Benny's, he found a noisy group of men he knew from the picket line.

"I didn't expect to find you guys here," he declared. "I thought for sure you'd be on your way home to Michigan as soon as you got outta jail."

"We only got out an hour ago," Buck said, "and we'd be gone if our bus had been waiting. But it won't be here 'til tomorrow."

"Haven't we seen you before?" someone asked.

"Yeah," Jerome said. "You seen me on the picket line."

"Did you rally with us, too?" Buck asked. "I mean, at the man camp on Saturday"

Jerome remembered seeing Buck moments after Hank, going in the wrong direction, shuffled past. Jerome wore a ski mask and was pretty sure that Hank hadn't recognized him. Buck was with the group that put the guard down, after which Jerome followed Buck and the the others to the trailers.

Jerome pulled a chair back and sat across from Buck. Debbie poured his shot of Jamison. He gave her a wink, tossed it and reached a hand to Buck.

"Name's Jerome. Some call me Jerry. I been on the picket line from the beginning, mostly during the week, but sometimes on the weekend, too.`

"I'm Buck Saari, from Michigan."

They shook hands.

"Were you at the man camp on Saturday?" Buck asked again.

"I was there, but I didn't go inside," Jerome said. "I have to be careful 'cause I'm on probation and the cops were there. They might've recognized me."

Buck waved to Debbie and pointed at Jerome's empty shot glass. He wondered how much the police observed from their vantage on the other side of the downed fence. He was relieved that Roger had kept quiet about the Packer jersey.

"What did you do outside of the man camp?" Buck asked.

"I watched the fence go down. It was almost like there was nothing holding it up. I saw everyone go in and I figured the scabs were going to take a beating. I heard after that no scabs were there."

"All we found was trailers," Buck said. "No scabs. Just empty trailers."

Jerome fled the camp while helicopters were hovering overhead. On his way out, he saw that the guard was still on the ground. "I heard that one of the guards got beat up. Do they know who done it?"

"We're charged with being in a riot," Buck said. "We don't know about any guard getting hurt. Where'd you hear about a guard?"

"It's been on the news," Jerome replied. "They say that he's in the hospital. The cops are asking anyone who seen what happened to come forward."

Someone went to the jukebox, dropped in some coins and returned to the sound of Johnny Cash.

"Speaking of Folsom Prison," Jerome said, "did anyone get arrested for arson? I saw lots of smoke coming from the trailers."

"We don't know about any fires, either" Buck said. "It might have been the teargas canisters that caused the fires. But the judge said that just for bein' in the riot, we could get a year in jail. We're gonna need a good lawyer."

"You only need a lawyer if you come back here from Michigan," Jerome said.

An anonymous caller gave Ted Grissom the name of the International Falls motel where he was to pick up his passengers. They would be some of the men who had been removed from his bus and detained several days earlier. Grissom had to cancel a charter in order to make another trip to Minnesota. He charged extra for the inconvenience. Once again, he did not ask where the money was coming from or who would be delivering it. The shuttle between Michigan and Minnesota was becoming a steady source of income. That was all he needed to know.

Early in the morning on Wednesday, Grissom parked behind the motel. His passengers didn't keep him waiting. Unlike the bus ride that brought fifty rowdy travelers to InternationalFalls from Michigan, this trip was a sober event. Having spent three nights behind bars and a fourth in crowded motel rooms, Grissom's passengers spoke with hushed voices, stared silently at the passing landscape or slept. When they reached Iron Mountain, Frank was there to greet them. He shook hands as they got off the bus, and he watched them hurry to their cars and pickup trucks. When all were gone, he went aboard the idling bus and put a paper bag with cash on the dashboard. He did not introduce himself to Grissom.

After weeks of late night movies watched from his bed in the intensive care unit, a simple message was indelibly etched in Tyrone's brain:

"Call Sam toll free. No recovery, no fee."

The words, accompanied by a confident and empathetic smile, were a constant reminder of what Tyrone had to do if and when he recovered.

The lawyer's mantra stayed with him during weeks of in-patient physical therapy, after which it followed him to a rented room where the sounds of bawling infants, hallway squabbles and toilets flushing made days indistinguishable from nights. When his therapist told him that his condition was as good as it was ever going to get, it was time to take action. Tyrone cashed his latest disability check, hitched a ride to Duluth in an Alderton Security van and bought a bus ticket to Minneapolis, where he checked into a motel. In his room, he fingered through a telephone directory until he found Sam Cramer's full page smile and the phone number that he knew by heart. He was a few minutes by taxi from Cramer's downtown office and he scrawled the address on a note pad before he picked up the phone and dialed.

The next morning, well before his nine-thirty appointment, Tyrone was in Sam Cramer's waiting room. While he leafed through an outdated Sports Illustrated, a secretary brought him coffee. A morning newscast from a television in a corner was telling viewers that traffic on Interstate 94 east of Minneapolis was backed up for several miles due to an accident.

"It's that way almost every morning," the secretary said from her desk. "They really ought to do something about it."

Tyrone stared at her and wondered who "they" were. She blushed and returned to her typing and he went back to his magazine just as the weather forecast came on. At exactly ten o'clock, she got up from her desk, beckoned and he followed her to Sam Cramer's private office.

"This is Mister Gates," she announced with a tight smile when they entered. "Tyrone Gates. He's here to see you about …"

"I know why he's here," Cramer interrupted. "You told me when you gave him the appointment. He's here about an injury. Have a seat Mister Gates, or may I call you Tyrone?"

"You can call me whatever you like if I can call you Sam, like on the television."

The secretary left the room, taking her smile with her until she was out of sight. Cramer smiled and motioned for Tyrone to be seated. Tyrone set his pair of canes down on one of the two chairs facing Cramer's desk and sat on the other.

The lawyer's shirt collar was open, exposing a thick gold chain that Tyrone did not remember from the television ads. He also was certain he had not seen the ornate rings that adorned several of Sam's fingers. He guessed that the watch was a Rolex. Cramer had a wide face, fleshy jowls and a square chin. He looked older in person than he did on television. His forehead was creased and his shiny brown hair, stylishly coiffed, showed no hint of gray. Tyrone decided that Sam was wearing a rug.

"Your television ads say I don't have to pay you unless you get some money for me," Tyrone began. "How does that work?"

Cramer's smile broadened. "You get right to the point. I like that." His smile faded. "I get a third plus my costs."

"What're your costs?"

"Filing fees, witness fees, court reporters, that sort of thing."

"Sounds like a lot. How much do you figure it's gonna be?"

"It's too soon to tell."

"One more question," Tyrone said. "Do you get your third before or after you take your costs?"

Cramer pretended not to have heard as he reached for a folder. He removed a printed form and handed it to Tyrone.

"My standard retainer agreement. Take your time and read it before you sign."

Tyrone studied it for a moment and handed it back. "Before I sign, let me tell you about my case."

Chapter Twenty-five

It was dark on the street except for the light shining from the windows of Lulu's Cafe. A brief thaw raised hopes for an early spring, but patches of ice remained where snow had been banked against the curbing. Inside the cafe, Jack Ross sat with Chief Patterson at the counter. The tables and booths behind them, on which Wanda was setting utensils wrapped in paper napkins, were unoccupied. The jukebox was silent. In half an hour, early breakfast regulars, mostly shift workers from the mill, would begin to arrive. When the Chief set his cup down and turned to speak to Jack, Wanda paused and listened.

" Except for Boise-Cascade's expansion, which is almost complete, local construction seems to be at standstill. Is there anything on the horizon? Do expect there will be work when the weather breaks?

Jack took a sip of coffee. It was hot but weak. Edith's was better.

"BE&K actually hired a couple of my local ironworkers last fall," he replied," but they were let go as soon as it was found out they were union."

"How did BE&K find out they were union?"

"Loose talk, I suppose. The company has its spies. I filed charges and the labor board is looking into it."

"What about the men that went to jail after the riot? Have you been able to find work for them?"

 There's been no work around here. Besides, everyone in Minnesota knows who they are. I'll have to send them out of the state."

A chill blew in from the street. Hank Peterson slipped off a quilted jacket and hung it near the door. "Mornin' Chief," he said when he reached the counter. "Mornin' Jack."

"Mornin,' they echoed.

Wanda poured Hank's coffee and freshened the others' cups.

"Can I get you anything else?"

"No thanks," Hank said. "I already had breakfast. Coffee's fine."

The Chief put a hand on Hank's shoulder. "You're up early for someone who doesn't have to be at work. I don't suppose you've retired?"

"I might as well be retired.There ain't any jobs around here."

"You could apply to work atE&K?" The Chief teased.

"BE&K knows I'm a union man."

"How do they know?" The Chief asked.

"Cuz I told 'em I was."

"Why did you do that?"

"Cuz they asked me. I knew they would, and I wasn't gonna lie."

"When did this happen?" Jack butted in.

"Just this past week. I heard that a couple of southerners spiked the job and left for home, so I asked for an application. I guess you can file another charge with the labor board."

"Fill me in on the details of what happened and I'll fill out a charge and send it in."

The Chief stood. "It's time for me to go to work. I'm on days."

"You're always on days," Hank said. "You're the Chief."

They watched him slip his coat on at the door. Wanda waited for Hank and Jack to drink more coffee so she could pour. When they didn't, she moved out from behind the counter.

"The picket line has been gone since the riot. There's no work around here except for BE&K, and my unemployment has run out," Hank said. "That's why I tried to sign on."

"It's okay," Jack said. "If you had been hired by BE&K, I would have understood. That's just the way things are."

"BE&K won't hire union ironworkers," Hank went on, "but they bring people up from the south that hasn't any experience. They get trained on the job. But I did hear a few union electricians got hired."

"Where did you hear that?"

"The electricians told me that BE&K had to have some electricians with Minnesota licenses. It's the law. The scab electricians don't have licenses."

"Are the union electricians from around here?"

"A couple of 'em are. I bet they have BE&K worried, too. But that doesn't help the rest of us who don't need licenses. BE&K won't hire us."

"As soon as we finish our coffee we'll file your complaint with the labor board."

Shift workers began to file in and sit at tables. Jack and Hank swung around on their stools to face them. "How are things at the mill?" Jack asked.

"Same old same old," was the answer.

"Where are all the new paper-making jobs ?" Hank asked. "That was part of the deal Boise made to get you guys to sign a contract? The new mill will be up and running soon. When is Boise going to start hiring?"

"Boise stuck it to us. There won't be anywhere near the number of new jobs that Boise promised."

"Boise stuck it to all of us," Hank said, "but at least you have jobs."

Jack got up and put on his coat. Hank followed him out. Later that morning, Hank's signature was on an unfair labor practice complaint.

"One more for the labor board," Jack told Edith when he was home "The strike may not have won the war, but the Rat will think twice before bidding on any more work in Minnesota."

"It wasn't much of a war," Edith said, "but at least it's over. Would you like a beer with your dinner?"

When traveling, Harlan Dixon preferred solitude with his meals. He also relished a good night's sleep on fresh linens. He told Conrad Jorgensen that he intended to have dinner before boarding his late afternoon flight from Birmingham. Jorgensen could wait. That evening, the BE&K vice president dined in his Minneapolis hotel room. That morning, he slept late. When he arrived at Jorgensen's office,, the instant coffee was tepid and bland, and he set his cup aside after a few sips.

"I want the Michigan ironworkers' union held fully accountable. Make it pay for every bit of damage that was done."

"That won't be difficult," the lawyer replied. "The leaflet ties the union to the riot like a ball and chain. What about the individual rioters, the ones that were convicted? Most of them entered guilty pleas. Their admissions of guilt are all the evidence I need."

"Easy to prove, but not easy to collect. You will have enough hours to bill without having to chase transient construction workers. Reach into the deeper pocket of the union. Go after its bank accounts, insurance and other assets."

"Right," Conrad agreed. "The union is the target. I'll get started right away."

"You can file a lawsuit in Minnesota and serve it on the ironworkers in Michigan," Dixon said. "That will send a message to other unions too."

"I'll file as soon as Sam Cramer finishes taking depositions."

"Who is Sam Cramer?" Dixon asked, "and what depositions are you talking about?"

" According to recent news accounts, Cramer is the lawyer who represents the guard that was injured during the riot. He has filed a lawsuit against the union and has begun subpoenaing witnesses."

"What does that have to do with us?"

"I can use Cramer's depositions to prepare. Once a witness tells his story to Cramer, I can order a copy of the deposition and look for weaknesses to attack when I examine the witness under oath."

Dixon disagreed. "Let's not give this Cramer fellow a head start. Get to the witnesses before he has a chance to mess things up."

Dixon removed a document from his briefcase and set it on Jorgensen's desk. He turned to the final page and took out a pen.

"Your retainer agreement has too much 'Whereas' and not enough 'Therefore' but I'll sign it anyway. Just be sure to get the results for which we are going to be paying you."

He stood and crossed the room to inspect Jorgensen's collection of certificates and celebrity photographs. One of the photos hung lightly askew and he straightened it before turning to face the lawyer.

"Now that the voters have had a chance to read his lips, do you think he might get a second term as President?"

"No doubt about it," Conrad replied, "especially if the Democrats are foolish enough to nominate that upstart from Arkansas."

They adjourned for cocktails and an early lunch at a nearby chophouse. Dixon was buying.

Frank LeClaire had all but forgotten about the riot until he received back-to-back wakeup calls. Suit papers prepared by Sam Cramer arrived in the morning mail, certified and with a return receipt for Frank's signature. Two days later, Frank was served with a second lawsuit, this one filed by Jorgensen.

"Cramer's suit says his client 'was beaten by union rioters'" Frank said, sitting in Ernie's office. "He says the injuries are 'serious and permanent.'"

"And 'disabling,'" Ernie added while reviewing the documents Frank handed him. "Cramer doesn't say how much money he wants for his client, but BE&K is asking for three million."

Ernie looked at Buck:

"You were there. Did it look to you that the riot caused that much damage to the man camp?"

"It might have. But if it did, why did it take so long for BE&K to sue?"

"BE&K had a project to complete,"Ernie said, "It put the lawsuit on hold. Now that the project is finished, it's payback time. But a three million dollar lawsuit probably inflates the amount of BE&K's loss."

"What about the guard?" Frank asked. "Why did he wait this long?"

"Before suing, a lawyer would want to know as much as possible about the nature of his client's injuries, the length of treatment and prognosis. The complaint says that Gates spent months in a hospital before being placed on a regime of out-patient therapy. Cramer also claims that Gates may never return to gainful employment. "

"Isn't there a statute of limitations?"Frank asked.

"Both lawsuits were filed within Minnesota's time limits. I looked it up."

"What do you know about the lawyers?" Frank asked. Jack Ross drew a blank on Conrad Jorgensen, but he called Cramer an ambulance chaser who advertises on television."

"I don't know anything about either one," Ernie replied. "I'll ask Mark Murphy what he knows about them.A lot of lawyers advertise on television these days. It's perfectly legit. While I'm at it, I'll also ask Murphy to file answers to these complaints."

"Aren't you going to represent us?"

"I would have to become licensed to practice law in Minnesota. I suppose Mark could sponsor me. Even so, you'll want to use him as local counsel."

"Doesn't that mean I'll have to pay for two lawyers?"

"Using Murphy will save money," Ernie explained. "He can handle routine matters in International Falls. I can do some of the heavy lifting from here, unless you prefer to pay me to commute between Michigan and Minnesota, which will add quite a few hours to my bill."

"Ouch," Frank winced." So tell me. How does it look? I mean, what are our chances?"

"It's too soon," Ernie said.

"How can the union be held responsible for what some of its members did?"

"That may depend on how one views a single piece of evidence."

"It wasn't supposed to leave my office."

"That's an argument I may have to sell. Got any others?"

"Don't look at me," Buck protested. "I saw it when I was in the office. I didn't see it again until it showed up at Quinnisec."

"You distributed copies at Quinnisec," Ernie said.

"I found them on the seat of my truck. I assumed that Frank changed his mind."

"You could've asked," Frank said"

"I didn't see any reason to ask. Why else would they be in my truck if you didn't want them handed out?"

"What's done is done," Ernie said. "I can't change the facts. I can only spin them."

"What happens next?" Frank asked.

"Depositions, record disclosures, preliminary motions and who knows what else. If I can't, come up with a winning explanation for the leaflet,settling these cases might be your best option."

Buck leaned close to Ernie: "Ironworkers don't settle with the Rat."

Chapter Twenty-six

Jerome was wide awake and staring at the darkness above his bed. He was trying to remember why he had been in the alley where he had been arrested. There was no denying that he was drunk, which left him without a defense to the charge of being a disorderly person. Now, after thirty days of jailhouse sobriety, he was on probation and was expected to remain sober or be remanded to the jail to serve the balance of his ninety day sentence.

Jerome had given his wife no explanation for his incarceration. She disappeared while he was waiting to be sentenced. His mother-in-law professed ignorance about her daughter's whereabouts. but Jerome had doubts. He also had only seventeen dollars and change from his final unemployment check, and his food supply was down to a half-empty package of saltines and a can of sardines. Worse, he was out of bourbon. There was also the matter of the subpoena that was handed to him earlier in the day, even though he was a millwright, never had been to Michigan and did not know anyone by the name of Tyrone Gates.

Jerome needed something to calm his nerves. He slid out of bed, put on street clothes and drove to Benny's Saloon. He hoped to find Debbie with few customers or, better yet, alone. As he came through door, he saw the uniform and stiffened although the officer's back was turned. Jerome didn't think the officer had seen him in the mirror behind the bar, but Debbie had seen him and he let the door close behind him.

Several women were sitting at a table. Jerome did not know them and could not think of no plausible excuse to join them. Officer Carmody was sitting alone at the bar. He had loosened his tie, his shirt collar was unbuttoned and his hat was next to his beer. Jerome, hoping to avoid eye contact, took a stool at the far end of the bar.

"The usual?" Debbie asked.

Jerome nodded and she filled a mug from a tap and brought it to him with the Jameson bottle and a shot glass. He glanced at the officer in the mirror while she poured. Carmody was not looking in Jerome's direction. So far, so good. When Debbie returned the bourbon to its shelf behind the bar, the mirror betrayed him. Jerome looked away, but it was too late.

"If I recall, Mister Banks, you were in a bit of trouble a while back," Carmody said. "I trust you've been on your best behavior since then. Maybe you should go easy on that hard stuff."

"I only stopped by for a nightcap," Jerome muttered.

He lifted the bourbon to his lips, set the empty shot glass down and stare at his mug of beer. Carmody get off his bar stool and moved to the stool next to Jerome. The women at the table paid no attention.

"What keeps you up at this late hour?" Carmody asked. "Just curious."

Jerome tried to come up with an answer. He was drinking in front of a cop, and not just any cop. He and this cop had a history.

"My shift ended, Carmody said."The wife and kids are visiting her folks in Grand Rapids. You're married, too, if I recall. Got any kids?"

Jerome accepted Carmody's outstretched hand and gave it a feeble shake.

"Yeah. I'm married, but no— no kids."

"'Last time I saw you was in court, wasn't it? You were given some jail time and probation. Right?

Jerome nodded.

"Don't worry. I'm not on duty and you appear to be sober. I would encourage you stay that way if you intend to drive after you leave. The night shift is on duty. "

"As soon as I finish my beer, I'll be on my way, but can I ask you something first'?"

"Shoot."

"Did you ever hear of anyone named Tyrone Gates?"

Carmody thought for a moment. "I can't say the name sounds familiar. I don't think I heard it before. What about this Tyrone. What's his last name?"

"Gates. I got a subpoena that has his name on it. A Michigan ironworkers union's name is on it, too. It says I'm to show up for a deposition."

"Who issued the subpoena?"

"I don't now. I suppose it was some lawyer, maybe for this Tyrone Gates or for the union. But why would anyone want me for a deposition? I got nothin' to do with either of them as far as I know."

"Maybe it has something to do with the strike at the mill. That was going on when you got into trouble, wasn't?"

"I picketed the construction. There's nothing wrong with that."

"You know what trouble I'm talking about."

"Yeah. I got arrested for being drunk. I didn't deny it, but I never met any Tyrone Gates, at least, not that I can recall."

"You mentioned ironworkers. There were ironworkers arrested during the riot and went to jail. Some of them were from Michigan."

"That's ancient history. Why would I be getting a subpoena now?"

"Property was destroyed during the riot and a security guard was injured and had to be taken to the hospital. Were you at the man camp?"

"I had nothin' to do with the riot. All I know is what I heard after. Do you think I should get a lawyer?"

"If you weren't at the man camp, why worry?"

"It's just that I never been at a deposition before. Maybe I'll say something to get me in trouble."

Carmody shrugged. The women at the table got up and began putting on sweaters and jackets. There was a chorus of "goodnight, Deb" and "See ya later," as they made for the door. Debbie came to check on the drinks at the bar. Carmody got off his stool and lifted his cap.

"I'll pass," he said. "It's time for me to get some shuteye."

He put a hand on Jerome's arm. "Maybe you should call it a night, too. You don't want to be caught violating your probation."

"I'm almost finished with my beer. Soon as I'm done, I'm out'a here."

Debbie rolled her eyes. Jerome's eyes followed Carmody to the door. When the officer was gone, Debbie began wiping the bar.

"You want another?" she asked, hoping he would decline.

"Might as well. One more won't hurt."

"You want another shot, too?"

"That's what I meant," he said. "One more and another beer."

She poured his shot, filled a mug and took her rag to the end of the bar.

"Can I buy you one?" he asked.

"No thanks," she replied.

"What are you doin' way over there? Come sit by me."

She hesitated, but came and sat next to him and watched him down the shot and begin to drain his beer.

"You married?" he asked.

"Divorced."

"I'm married, but I don't know for how long. My wife left me."

"I know. You told me that before."

"She's disappeared," he said. "Even her mom don't know to where she went."

"Sorry to hear it."

"You got plans for tonight? I hate to go home alone."

"Don't get any ideas."

"You sure?"

"I'm sure. Drink up. It's closing time."

The sun was rising when Sam Cramer left his suburban Minneapolis home. He looked forward to the five hour drive north as an opportunity for serious reflection, but his mind wandered. Long before he reached InInternational Falls, he was thinking about lunch. Seated in a booth at Lulu's Cafe, sipping his coffee and reading a day-old newspaper while waiting for a grilled ham and cheese, he was vaguely aware that the room was filling with a noonday crowd. He paid no attention to two men who were chatting with the waitress at the counter.

Jerome and Hank were telling Wanda about their subpoenas. When their cups were empty, she poured more coffee and moved out from behind the counter , order pad in hand. Sam thought he heard mention of his client and looked up. Jerome was gesturing with his hands, but the conversation at the counter was inaudible over the chatter around him the music from the juke box. Leaving a dollar bill on the table, he got up and went to the cash register to wait for Wanda to bring his check. The two sitting at the counter were still talking and juke box was still playing when he left.

On the sidewalk outside, Sam buttoned his coat, turned up this collar and hurried to his car. If Mark Murphy's office were in Minneapolis, where it was fifteen degrees warmer, he would have walked. But his car was still warm. When he arrived at Murphy's office, a secretary took his coat and directed him to a seat in the waiting room.

"Mister Murphy hasn't returned from lunch," she said, "but I expect him to be back any minute. Would you like coffee while you wait?"

He thanked her, but declined. If Murphy was having lunch at Lulu's he would be wearing a suit and tie. Sam could not recall seeing anyone dressed like a lawyer. As he reached to pick up a magazine, he heard female voices. He tried to listen, but the voices faded, then stopped. He put the magazine down and looked at his watch, wishing he had accepted the coffee.

A few minutes later, Mark's secretary reappeared. She led Sam to a room where a stenographer was setting up her recording equipment at a conference table. She was tall, blond and smartly dressed in a business outfit. Sam thought she was pretty and kept his eyes on her after he was seated. When Mark Murphy arrived with his client, introductions were made. Jerome winked at the stenographer who remained expressionless. Sam was certain that Jerome was one of the men at the lunch counter, but Murphy, who was wearing a suit, was not the other. Mark and Jerome took seats with Jerome nearest to the stenographer. When Sam signaled that he was ready, the stenographer asked Jerome to stand, raise his right hand and swear to tell the truth.

Chapter Twenty-seven

Hiram was able to salvage and sell enough parts from his battered and wrecked pickup truck to have money for bus fare to Alabama. He wrote to Betsy and told her that he expected his job to end soon. When he was handed his layoff notice, he wrote to her again and enclosed the schedules for the Greyhounds that would take him from Duluth to Minneapolis, to Birmingham and, finally, to Dothan. But when his final day of work arrived, he was offered an automobile ride to Nashville with three other laid off workers. He didn't have time to notify Betsy of his changed travel plans.

After he paid his share for gasoline, Hiram had enough money to buy meals at highway diners in rural Indiana, Kentucky and Tennessee. The meat patties were thin and tasteless, the buns were stale and the chicory-laced coffee was lukewarm and weak. He took solace from the knowledge that in a matter of days he would enjoy Betsy's home cooking. He tried to imagine how the children might look after growing and maturing during his absence. He wondered if they would respond to him as affectionately they had before the separation. Although he would have liked them be there to greet him upon his arrival in Dothan, he assumed that they would be in school. Nor would Betsy be greeting him. Since he would be arriving sooner than she had been told to expect him. He smiled at the thought of how surprised and pleased she would be.

When Hiram wasn't driving, he tried to sleep. His slumber was punctuated by stops for food, fuel and visits to roadside restrooms. In Nashville, he paced while waiting to board the bus to Birmingham where he would pace some more while waiting for the bus that would deliver him to his final stop. In Dothan, hailed a taxi and gave the driver the address that Betsy sent him when she wrote that she had moved from her mother's home to a furnished bungalow. When the taxi pulled to the curb in front of a single-story, shingle-sided residence, Hiram paid the driver and got out. Standing at the curb as the taxi drove off, he wore a puzzled expression. He reached into his shirt pocket and retrieved Betsy's letter— the one with her address. It matched the number on the house, but its windows were shuttered and the cement walk and front steps to the porch were littered with folded newspapers. In the center of a lawn overgrown with weeds was a sign that read, "For Rent."

"The agreement that we made allows Sam Cramer to take his depositions in Mark's office in International Falls," Ernie explained. "You and I will be attending from my office by speaker phone, but Buck wasn't included. I'll have to tell Cramer that he's in the room with us. If Cramer objects, Buck will have to leave."

Buck muttered something under his breath, Frank said nothing, and when the telephone rang at Kathy's desk in the outer office, she transferred the call to Ernie and he put the caller on speaker phone.

"Who's in the room with you?" Cramer asked.

Buck stood and threw up his hand.

"Frank LeClaire and Buck Saar are with me. Buck is here as a member of the union's executive board."

"Buck Saari participated in the riot. He was arrested, convicted and sentenced," Sam said. "That makes him a potential witness at trial. I thought we had an agreement—just you and the business manager."

"Are you objecting to Buck being here?" Ernie asked.

"You bet I'm objecting. Send him out or the deposition is off."

Ernie turned to Buck. "You'll have to wait in the outer office."

Buck rolled his eyes. "Lawyers," he muttered as he left the room.

"Buck has gone and I'm now' alone with Frank. Who's in the room with you?"

"Mark Murphy, the witness and the stenographer, just like we agreed. Are you ready to get started?"

"Ready whenever you are."

After being sworn, Jerome answered some preliminary questions, giving his name, address, date of birth and education. When asked to recite his employment history, he balked.

"I've worked everywhere in the midwest and in some western states, too. I go wherever the union sends me. Sometimes a job lasts a few days, sometimes for weeks. I can show you a stack of W-2s this high," he said, gesturing. "That's the only way I can give you the names of all the employers I worked for."

"Did you bring your W-2s with you?" Sam asked. "The subpoena said you were to bring them to the deposition."

"I guess I didn't read that part. But if you want me to, I can go home and get them. They'll only tell you who I worked for. They won't tell you the exact dates or where, and I won't be able to tell you either."

"The only place you're gonna find such detailed information," Frank broke in from Escanaba, "is in his fringe benefit records. I'm talking about pension contributions, health and welfare, that sort'a thing. You'll have to subpoena the fund administrators."

"If you wish," Ernie offered, "We can recess and wait while he goes home to look for his W-2s. For how many years back do you want them ?"

"I can return to this line of inquiry later," Sam said. "Let's move on."

Jerome acknowledged that in 1989 he had picketed with ironworkers and others at the Boise-Cascade construction gate. He said he didn't remember the name of anyone who came to picket from Michigan or any other state.

"I wasn't on the picket line every day. I was mostly there during the week and only sometimes on a weekend. The only ones picketing that I knew were from around here."

"By 'around here' do you mean International Falls?"

"Yeah. Here and places near here. Sometimes they were even from as far away as Duluth."

"What were the names of those who came from Duluth?"

"I might have known a few names back then, but I don't remember them as we sit here, today."

When asked if he had ever been convicted of a felony, Jerome looked at Murphy. Mark shook his head.

"I guess not," Jerome answered.

"Meaning 'no'?" Sam asked.

"Yeah. I mean no felony. Just disorderly."

"Were you in International Falls on September 9, 1989?"

"Yeah."

"Did you participate in a union-sponsored rally on that date?"

"Objection," Ernie shouted over the speaker phone. "The question assumes a fact not in evidence. You haven't established that whatever may have taken place on that date was sponsored by a union."

Before the words left his mouth, Ernie realized that the objection was pointless since this was a deposition, not a trial. "Subject to my objection, the witness may answer," he added.

Jerome looked at Mark who shrugged.

"I recall a crowd being there," Jerome said. "Basically, it was guys that were on strike and others who I didn't know. But yeah. I wast there that day and I guess you could call it a rally."

'How many of those others—the ones you didn't know—were there?"

"I can't say how many. But there was quite a few."

"Were any of them from Michigan?"

"Could have been. I can't say for sure. I only heard that some were from Michigan."

"Where did you hear that some were from Michigan? Who told you?"

Jerome paused, thinking.

"What did he say?" Ernie asked, leaning closer to the speaker phone. "I didn't hear his answer."

"He hasn't answered, yet," Sam said.

"I don't know where I heard it," Jerome said. "It was back then and I don't remember."

Sam removed a Manila envelope from his briefcase and withdrew several eight-and-a-half by eleven, black ad white photographs. He placed all but one face down on the table and handed the one to Jerome.

"Do you recognize the tall man wearing the jersey with hash marks?"

Jerome studied the photograph of Buck and several other men standing over a prone figure on the ground.

"Take whatever time you need," Sam said.

"What did you show him?" Ernie asked. "What's he looking at?"

"I gave him a photograph of some men, one of whom appears to be wearing an athletic team jersey. I asked him if he recognized him."

155

"I want to have a look at it, too," Ernie said. Have it marked as an exhibit, attach the original to the deposition transcript and send a copy to me by fax or mail."

"Answer the question," Sam said to Jerome. "Do you recognize this man?"

"I don't believe I seen him before," Jerome declared.

"Are you sure?"

"I'm pretty sure I never seen him."

Sam continued to hand photographs to Jerome. Many in the photographs wore ski masks. Jerome assumed they were from town and were hiding their identity from local law enforcement, just as he had done. A few who weren't masked were men from Michigan with whom he had picketed. Most were strangers.

"I can't honestly say I recognize any of these. There was lots of strangers in town that day."

Sam set the photographs aside. "Did you enter the man camp at any time on September 9, 1989?"

Murphy interrupted. "You don't have to answer. You have that right under the Fifth Amendment."

"No, he doesn't," Sam protested. "This is not a criminal proceeding."

"It doesn't matter," Mark insisted. "You are asking whether he did something that might be a crime. He can refuse to incriminate himself."

"You're obstructing my examination. I can get a court order."

"I'm not obstructing anything. I'm not even his lawyer. I represent the union. I'm just letting him know that he has the right to remain silent. Whether he wishes to exercise that right is up to him."

Jerome stared at the stack of photographs that remained face down. He had worn a ski mask, but he wasn't certain that it was foolproof.

"Yeah. I went into the man camp, but I got out as soon as I seen what was happening."

"How long were you in the man camp?"

"It wasn't very long. I just went in and turned around and left."

Sam handed Jerome a piece of paper. "Have you seen this before?"

Jerome studied it.

"Might have."

"Take your time. Think about it and tell me if you've seen it before."

"Maybe."

"Maybe what?"

"Maybe I seen it before."

"I'm not asking you to guess. Answer 'yes' or 'no'. Have you seen it before today?"

" I might have seen it or seen something like it. It's been a while."

"Tell me how you happened to see it or something like it."

"It could have been someone from Michigan who was on the picket line that showed it to me. It says right here that it's from the ironworkers union in Michigan."

"Do you remember who from the ironworkers union showed it to you?"

"Are you kidding? That was a couple years ago or more by now. How am I supposed to remember?"

"But could it have been an ironworker or someone from Michigan?"

"Of course it could've been. It says so right on it. But I can't say that whoever showed it to me was from Michigan. I don't recall who showed it to me."

Sam gave Jerome a photograph of Hank Peterson.

"Do you recognize the person in this photograph?"

Jerome looked at Murphy. Mark looked away.

"Sure. I know him. That's Hank Peterson. I know him pretty good. What of it?"

"Did you see him in the man camp during the riot on September 9, 1989? Let's call it a riot. That's what it was, wasn't it?

Mark Murphy objected. "Calls for an opinion."

"No foundation," Ernie added.

"I'll rephrase the question," said Cramer. "Did you see Hank Peterson in the man camp on September 9?"

"It looks like that might be where he was in the photo."

"My question was did you see him there that day?"

"I can't say. I was in, and I was out. I seen lots'a guys. I could've seen Hank and not even known it was him if he was wearing a mask. I can't say if I saw him or not."

As the deposition progressed, "I don't remember" was Jerome's response to most of Sam's questions, and Jerome's confidence grew in proportion to the lawyer's frustration.

"Can we agree that what happened on September 9, 1989 was violent and upsetting?"

"You could say that. Sure."

"Do you always have difficulty remembering violent and upsetting events?"

"Only when I been drinking."

"Were you drinking that day?"

"I don't remember."

Buck paced the floor in Erne's outer office, muttering to himself and setting Kathy's nerves on edge. She offered him coffee. He declined and she returned to her desk and tried to make sense of the document she had been typing. Buck's exclusion from the deposition as an insult compounded by his banishment to Ernie's outer office. It wasn't long before he slipped his coat on and left the building and walked the few short blocks to Escanaba's waterfront park. Ignoring the stiff breeze coming off of Little Bay de Noc, he sat on a bench facing the yacht harbor.

The fishing shanties of winter were gone, but chunks of ice remained along the shore. Geese were gathering on the lawn at the far end of the park. Buck wondered how long they would remain before continuing their northward migration. A slow-moving police cruiser passed by and the officer behind the wheel eyed the lone figure sitting near the water. Buck returned the officer's stare until the cruiser turned the corner onto Ludington Street and disappeared.

Images of the riot flashed through Buck's mind. Red and blue lights flashed while the uniformed police stood by their vehicles, making no effort to intercept the men who were charging into the man camp. When the guard appeared from nowhere and swung his flashlight, Buck managed to keep the old guy from falling before the guard was put down. When they put the boots to him, some had their faces covered. He thought that Roger Beaudre might have been one of them. Then they ransacked the trailers until the tear gas forced them out. Buck wondered whether the guard's injuries were as serious as the suit papers claimed, making it sound like he was crippled. He had been foolish as to pick a fight with an angry mob.

More geese glided to a soft landing near the others. Buck wondered how close they might let him approach before they challenged him. But it was cold, and he got up from his bench and walked back to Ernie's office.

Chapter Twenty-Eight

In the waiting room, Jerome gave a up toHank, whose hands were folded in his lap to keep them still. Hank responded with a nervous smile. This was his first deposition and a lawyer's office was only slightly less intimidating than the senior ironworker imagined a courtroom to be. He was told he would be asked to swear an oath to tell the truth and that he should be be wary because lawyers had ways of tricking you if you didn't pay close attention.

"Whenever possible, answer with a simple 'yes' or 'no," Mark Murphy had instructed him. "Do not volunteer information and, If you must explain, be brief and to the point."

The moment Jerome emerged from the conference room, Hank's pulse quickened. His palms felt damp and he wiped them on his trousers. His mouth was dry, when he reached for the glass of water the secretary brought him. It was his turn and he took deep breaths as he followed her. and focused on the words Jerome spoke as he was leaving:

"Piece 'a cake."

Jerome told Hank that they should stick up for one another because they were friends and had been on the picket line together. He said that Hank should say he didn't know who put the boots to the guard because that was what Hank had said when Jerome asked him. He said that it might have been the big guy in the Packer jersey, but he wasn't sure. There were others there, too. Jerome warned Hank that the lawyer might try to get him to change his mind and blame someone. Hank said he didn't see how he could be made to change his mind because he really didn't know.

Jerome parked his truck at the curb in front of his house, got out and studied the front yard. His wife was right. It was an eyesore, but he didn't care. He went to the front door, unlocked it and stepped inside. The room was littered with clothing waiting to be laundered—underwear, socks, a few of his shirts and jeans. He didn't care about that either. He didn't care about the empty bottles and cans or the newspapers that were strewn about the living and dining rooms. In the kitchen, there were dirty dishes on the table and in the sink. He had been meaning to wash and put them away, but he kept putting it off because he didn't care.

Upstairs in the bedroom, there were blankets and linens piled on the bed. The floor was littered with crumbs and other reminders of his late-night appetites. His mother-in-law's number was scrawled on a notepad beside the telephone on the nightstand next to the bed. He had given up calling her.

He went downstairs to the living room, and slumped onto a worn, overstuffed chair. He was staring at a blank television screen when the telephone rang. He let it ring five times before he picked it up.

"Jerome," he growled. "Who's calling?"

It was the business manager of his union.

"I got a call to send some millwrights to a job in North Dakota. They have to be in Grand Forks by Monday morning. You're on my list. Are you interested"

Jerome sat up.

"Tell me more."

"It's maintenance work at a power plant. Should be good for a couple weeks. Do you want it or not?"

After he put the phone down, Jerome began gathering things into a paper bag— a woman's watch, a pearl necklace and some costume jewelry. He looked for his wife's engagement ring. The small diamond was missing but he found her wedding band. It was gold. Maybe she forgot it. Maybe she left it behind for spite. He didn't care.

He wasn't in the pawn shop very long and he left disappointed. The pearls were fake, the wedding band wasn't gold and he wasn't in a position to haggle. The money he got would pay for a full tank of gas and there would still be enough for a shot and a beer before he left town. When he got to Benny's, Debbie was talking to a customer. The customer looked familiar and Jerome tried to remember where he had seen him before. When Debbie introduced them, Jerome scowled.

"I thought the Rat's work was finished," he said. "How come you're still in town?"

"My rent's paid to the end of the month and I'm waiting for another assignment," Mike Carr said. " I sent the family back to Indiana. My wife is from Fort Wayne. That's where I'll be, too, if I don't get an assignment before my next month's rent is due."

"Didn't you see the sign over the door?" Jerome asked. "This place is for union only."

"I took the sign down," Debbie said. She poured Jerome's shot and drew a beer from a tap.

"Why'd you take it down?" he asked. "You want scabs in here?"

"Get over it, Jerome. Almost everyone that came to work for BE&K is gone, but I still got a saloon to run. The Beaver Dam lost most of its business. If it closes, this' will be the only game in town. I don't want anyone to feel they ain't welcome."

"I just came from the Beaver Dam," Mike said. "It was closed."

"Today's a weekday," Debbie explained. "The Beaver Dam only opens Friday night for fish fries and Saturday afternoon and evening. I don't expect it to be in business much longer."

"Good riddance," Jerome exclaimed, "And good riddance to BE&K and its scabs."

Mike took that as his cue and paid his tab, leaving an extra dollar on the bar for Debbie.

"I'm out'a here, too, soon as I finish my beer," Jerome announced. "I'm goin' home to pack a suitcase and head to North Dakota."

Debbie gave him a curious look. Several men came in and sat at a table. Jerome greeted them by name and got off his stool. He sat with them and waited for someone to order a round.

Hank's voice cracked and he tried to clear his throat. He wondered why he had to spell his last name for the stenographer. He had known her since she was a child. Her father was his barber and her mother managed a local gift shop. He was about to ask her if there was more than one way to spell Peterson when Cramer asked him for his home address, date of birth, and the number of years he had lived in International Falls. By the time Sam got to education, vocational training and work experience, Hank was feeling more comfortably. When Sam finally began asking about the riot, Hank's palms were dry and he was no longer conscious of his heartbeat.

"You said that when you left home that day, you intended to go to the construction gate. What made you change your mind?"

Sam waited while Hank thought it over. Ernie thought he might have missed something. "What did he say?" he asked into the speaker phone.

"What did who say?" Sam replied. "Me or the witness?"

Before Ernie could respond, Hank gave his answer.

"When I pulled out of the driveway and got to the end of my street, there was a lot of traffic. It was mostly pickup trucks. They wasn't goin' in the direction of the gate. I thought that was odd, so I followed."

"To where?"

"To the man camp."

"Why did you follow them to the man camp?"

"'Cause that's where they was goin'."

"No, no. I mean what was your reason for following them. You said you were going to the construction gate?"

"I wanted to see what was up."

"Couldn't you tell what was up?"

"Not a clue."

"Okay. When you got to to the man camp, what did you do?"

"I parked and got out and and then I...."

Sam interrupted. "Tell me what you saw when you got out of your truck."

"There was pickup trucks and cars. I even seen a bus, or maybe it was two. And men was running toward the man camp."

"How many men?"

"I can't say how many. I didn't count them. I only know there was lots and they was running and shouting."

"Running.?"

"Yeah. Like I said—to the man camp. I followed. When I got there, the fence was down and there was men already inside."

"Did you go inside?"

Hank looked at Mark, hoping for a hint. Ernie, in Escanaba, waited for Mark to object, but he was writing something on a legal pad and didn't appear to have heard the question.

Hank thought about the men who had been jailed for their part in the riot. He had worked with some of them and had been with them on the picket line. What did it matter that following them had been a mistake? He had chosen sides.

"Yeah," he blurted. "I went into the man camp with the others."

"Do you know the names of any of the others who went in?"

Hank was pretty sure that he had seen Jerome wearing a ski mask and there might have been some others that he knew. He thought about the fallen guard. Was that when he saw Jerome? His palms felt moist again.

"I can't recall seeing anyone I knew. I might've, but I can't say for certain that I did. Some had their faces covered. The ones that didn't was mostly strangers. There were some who stayed outside the fence and didn't go in. I wasn't paying attention to who went in and who didn't."

"You said those without masks were 'mostly strangers. I want you to tell me who you saw that was without a mask and wasn't a stranger. Who were you able to recognize?"

Hank's mouth was dry. He heard himself say, "I don't remember seeing anyone I recognized. I didn't take time to look around. I just wanted to get away from there."

"Why?"

"Why what?"

"Why did you want to get away?"

"'Because I didn't belong there."

Hank knew he was giving evasive answers, but he seemed to be getting away with it.

"How well do you know Jerome Banks?" Sam asked.

Hank took a deep breath.

"We see each other now and then. I seen him here a few minutes ago."

"Did you see him that day in the man camp?"

"I won't say I actually saw him there, but I can't say for sure he wasn't. He could've been.

Murphy interrupted.

"If you don't know the answer to a question, just say you don't know. You don't have to speculate."

Hank didn't want to lie, but he couldn't tell them that he thought Jerome might have been one of the men he saw kicking the guard. They were wearing ski masks. Maybe it wasn't Jerome. How could he be certain if he didn't see his face?

"I don't know if Jerome was there or not."

Cramer sighed. "Okay. Tell me what you did inside the man camp."

"I followed the others in, but soon's I saw what they was doin', I was gonna turn to go back out. That's when I got hit."

"We'll get to that," Cramer said, picking up a photograph and showing it to Hank. "Do you recognize anyone in this picture?"

Over the speaker phone, Ernie said "Mark it as an exhibit and see that I get a copy."

"That looks like me from behind," Hank said, pointing. It must've been before I got hit 'cuz you can see some smoke over by the trailers. I was goin' in that direction before I turned around to go other way."

"How about the person behind you on the right? He's only partly visible, but can you tell me who that is?"

"Looks like he's wearing a uniform. If he is, he'd be one of the guards. He could even be the one that hit me."

"You say a guard hit you? Was it with a fist?"

"I'm guessing it was a guard. But It was heavier than a fist. It felt pretty hard."

"You didn't see who or what it was that hit you?"

"Never did."

Sam showed Hank another photograph.

"Tell me what you see in this photo."

"That looks like me after I got hit, but I can't tell you who it was that grabbed me."

Cramer showed Hank a photograph of several men standing over a figure on the ground. Hank studied it.

"Does that look familiar?" Sam asked.

"It does."

"Tell me what's familiar about it."

165

"When I got hit, I almost went down. I looked to see who it was that kept me from falling. That's when I seen some guys,— it was more than just one or two— that was kicking someone on the ground."

"Do you know who was on the ground?"

"Not really. It might've been the guard 'cause I remember a uniform and that looks like it in the picture, too. But I'm just sayin' it might be. And if you ask me who was kicking him, I don't know that either cuz I didn't stick around. I got out'a there quick as I could."

"A moment ago you said you decided to leave when you saw what others were doing."

"That's right."

"And in a previous photograph you recognized the smoke that was coming from a trailer."

"Yeah."

"That was before you got hit?"

"That's how I remember it."

"And that was also before you saw men kicking someone. You must have been in the man camp for quite a while ."

"Was that a question?" Mark Murphy asked.

"Withdrawn," Sam said, adding, "I have nothing further."

He began sliding photographs into his briefcase. Hank felt a rush of relief. The stenographer started to review her notes. Mark stood, stretched and asked Hank to remain seated until Cramer was gone.

"Is there anything you need from Mister Peterson before he leaves?" Mark asked into the phone.

"Not that I can think of," Ernie replied.

"I hope I didn't get anyone in trouble," Hank said before Kathy shut the speaker phone off in Escanaba.

Chapter Twenty-nine

While Jack Ross was hanging his jacket in the front hallway closet, Edith was telling him about the process server that had been to the house earlier in the day.

"He said he had court papers for you."

"You didn't accept them, did you?"

"I told him you left town and don't live here anymore."

"Good girl."

"I don't think he believed me. Why would he looking for you?"

"Frank LeClaire's union is being sued and Frank has been subpoenaed to give a deposition. He said I'd probably get a subpoena, too. I'm playing hard to get."

"If that process server returns, he'll see your camper in the driveway. Maybe you should park it somewhere else."

"I'll be leaving first thing in the morning. I'm going where they won't think of looking for me."

"Where's that?"

"Never mind. If anyone asks for me , tell them you don't know where I am."

"How long will you be gone?"

"Hard to say. Process servers will be turning Minnesota upside down trying to find me. You could tell them I'went fishing, but you don't know what lake. That'll keep 'em busy for a while."

"I already told one you don't live here any more."

"You said he probably didn't believe you."

In the morning, Jack's camper was gone. That afternoon, it was parked several blocks from Frank's office in Marquette.

"You must be crazy," Frank exclaimed. "BE&K's lawyer is upstairs right now. He's taking Buck's deposition. He has people looking everywhere for you. If he finds out you're here…"

"Everyone thinks I'm in Minnesota. Nobody will be looking for me here. Even if the lawyer sees me, he won't know who I am. He doesn't know what I look like. When he's finished upstairs, you can buy dinner."

In the meeting room above them, Buck refused to testify.

"The Fifth Amendment doesn't apply," Jorgensen argued. "You've already served six months for your part in the riot. Once you've been convicted, you can't be placed in jeopardy again. I can take you into court. The judge will order you testify or be sent to jail for contempt."

Buck stood firm, Ernie shrugged. Jorgensen repeated the threat to no avail. Buck was dismissed and it was Frank's turn to testify.

"Did you prepare a leaflet urging union members to take part in a rally at International Falls on September 9, 1989?"

"I did."

Jorgensen marked a copy of the leaflet as an exhibit and Frank identified it as the one he prepared.

"To whom did you give copies?"

"I never."

"You never what?"

"I never gave copies to anyone."

"Who gave copies to the workers at the paper mill site in Quinnisec, Michigan?"

"Don't know."

"You don't know, or are you refusing to tell me?"

"I said I didn't know, and even if I did know I wouldn't tell you. It's none of your business. Ask me something else.

"Let's take a break," Ernie broke in "A couple minutes."

Jorgensen did not object, and in the hallway, Ernie stood facing Frank.

"Let's get one thing straight. I am the lawyer. You are the witness. You don't get to argue with the other lawyer. That's my job. Your job is to answer questions. Do your job and let me do mine. *Capiche?*"

Frank returned to the witness chair, Ernie returned to his seat next to him at the table and Conrad continued.

"If you didn't show the leaflet to anyone, what did you do with it."

Ernie interrupted.

"He never said he didn't show it to anyone. He said he didn't give it to anyone. He showed it to me."

"What was Mister Hunter's response when you showed him the leaflet?"

"Objection. Attorney-client privilege. I'm instructing him to not answer."

"Fine. Have it your way," Jorgensen stammered, "but remember, two can play that game."

Ernie couldn't tell if Jorgensen meant that as a threat. Conrad wasn't certain either.

"He's already admitted that he prepared the leaflet," Jorgensen continued. "I want to know what he did with it."

"I didn't do anything with it," Frank replied. "It was supposed to be shredded."

"What do you mean by 'supposed to be? Was it shredded or wasn't it?"

"It should have been. I thought it was. Apparently, it wasn't."

"Did you make copies?"

"Did not."

"Who did?"

"Don't know. My secretary could have, but she says she didn't."

"Who besides you and your secretary could have made copies?"

Frank shrugged.

In L'Anse, Michigan, Nick Beaudre asked his father why he had waited so long to come home after he got out of jail?"

"I was ashamed," Roger began." It was something I wasn't ready to talk about."

He paused, trying to find the right words—- words for which he had been searching for months.

"I went to International Falls to take part in a rally. We were there to protest work being done by scabs— non-union labor."

"I know what scabs are," Nick said, "but why were you in jail?"

"I thought we'd be going to the construction gate where we had been picketing. Instead, we were let off where the scabs were housed. It was a Saturday. Whoever was leading the charge must have thought the scabs would be at the camp."

"Were they?"

"That was the strange part. There was nobody there except a few security guards."

"If the scabs had been there, were you going to beat 'em up?"

"Probably. But we never …"

"Okay. So you went to the camp and no one was there. Then what happened?"

"We tore the fence down and went in . We wrecked things."

"What things? Was that why you were arrested?"

"Cars, trucks, anything we could get our hands on. We even tipped a bus over and someone began setting things on fire. I had nothing to do with setting fires."

"Why didn't you leave when you saw what was happening?"

"It happened too fast. I was with an angry mob and I became a part it. By the time I realized what we were doing, it was too late to back out. I know that sounds dumb, but that's how it was."

Roger decided to not tell Nick about the guard.

"I served my time, and I just want things to be like they were before."

Frank continued to give Conrad Jorgensen the same answers he had given to Ernie.

"I don't know how the leaflet got out of my office. I left it on my desk. Members are in and out all the time, asking about work, insurance benefits, pensions. Anyone could have taken it."

He didn't know if Ernie believed him, and he doubted that Jorgensen did.

"Wouldn't you or your secretary have seen or heard if someone were made copies of the leaflet in your office?" Conrad had asked.

"Maybe. But copies also could've been made somewhere else."

"Are you saying that's what happened?"

"No. I'm just saying maybe that's what happened."

"Do you ever leave your office unattended?"

"My secretary is usually there when I'm not, but sometimes our lunch breaks overlap. Sometimes the door may be left locked."

"Sometimes?"

"Not always. But it's possible that it's sometimes it's left unlocked."

Jorgensen asked about the money Frank used to help members post bond.

"You already now that I took out a personal loan. The bank gave you copies of the records. You subpoenaed them."

'Have you repaid the loan?"

"Every penny."

"According to the union's payroll records, you don't earn enough to repay such a large loan in so little time."

"The members took up collections on various jobs."

"In cash?"

"Yeah. Cash."

"Did you keep a record of who gave money and how much?"

"Didn't need to. It wasn't union business. It was personal"

"Who paid for the bus that took your members to International Falls?"

"I don't know that, either."

"Didn't the union pay for the bus?"

"Nope. You subpoenaed the union's bank records, too."

AfterFrank's deposition ended, he and Ernie remained in the room while Jorgensen questioned Ted Grissom.

"Who hired you to drive your bus from Michigan to International Falls on September 9, 1989?"

"The voice on the phone said he was a concerned citizen."

"Be more specific. Give me a name."

"Can't. All he said was 'concerned citizen.'"

"How were you paid?"

"Cash."

"Who paid you?"

"Don't know."

"How could you not know who paid you? Money doesn't materialize out of thin air. You must have some idea."

"When this concerned citizen called, I gave him a price and told him he'd have to pay before I left for International Falls. The money was in a paper bag on the dashboard of my bus. I never saw who put it there."

"Did you ask anyone if they knew who left the money?"

"Who was I gonna ask? No one was on the bus but me when I found the money and counted it."

Jorgensen did not know that Grissom made a second trip to International Falls to retrieve the Michigan riders after they were released on bond. When Conrad could think of nothing more to ask, Ernie said he had no questions and the deposition was over.

It was after five o'clock. Frank's secretary had left the office.

"Let's walk over to the Shamrock," Frank suggested. "I asked Buck to wait for us there. Jack Ross may waiting for us, too."

They found a table and ordered a round of drinks. Buck and Jack, who were sitting at he bar, joined them.

"What happens now?" Frank asked. "How long do you think it will be before we go to trial?"

"If we go to trial," Ernie corrected him. "You prepared the leaflet. That much has been established. What makes you think a jury will believe that you weren't responsible for distributing it?"

"Do you believe me?"

"Whether I believe you isn't the issue. The only thing that will matter is whether a jury believes you."

'What's the worst case scenario?"

"Based on BE&K's property damage and loss appraisals, the union could be tagged for a million dollars, give or take. As for Gates, he may never be able to work again. Add pain and suffering to his loss of income, and a jury could render a verdict that would be disastrous."

Chapter Thirty

Harlan Dixon flew to Minneapolis from Birmingham. Ernie and Frank made the trip from Escanaba in Ernie's automobile. When everyone was seated at the table in Conrad Jorgensen's conference room, the meeting began.

"Although I notified the court's scheduling clerk that I'm ready for trial," Jorgensen began "the judge sent word that wants us to try to settle the case before he sets a trial date. Frankly, I see no reason for BE&K to settle for anything less than what it has demanded in its complaint. I have the leaflet, and my damage appraisals support a substantial verdict. That leaves me with little or no incentive to negotiate "

"'There's bound to be at least one or two union members on the jury," Ernie said. "They're not going to reward BE&K for bringing scab labor to Minnesota. Your out-of state client took jobs that should have gone to local building tradesmen. BE&K's anti-union tactics are not going to find a sympathetic audience in a Minnesota courtroom."

"I doubt that law-abiding jurors, including those who sympathize with unions, will have much sympathy for a Michigan union that sent its thugs to incite a riot in Minnesota," Jorgensen countered.

Ernie had cautioned Frank that a BE&K victory might be used by Sam Cramer to leverage Tyrone Gates' case against the union. Dual losses could spell doom for the union. On the other hand, Jorgensen had to admit, if only to Dixon, that a few of his loss appraisals were inflated which,. if exposed at trial, would undermine the credibility of accurate appraisals. Dixon also knew that most of the property in question had been fully depreciated for tax purposes, reducing BE&K's actual loss to something far less than it was claiming.

Dixon had a plane to catch and he asked the lawyers to excuse themselves so that he and Frank could meet privately. Jorgensen felt slighted, Ernie was grateful for the reprieve and both lawyers left the room. When they reached Jorgensen's office, Ernie asked for directions to a restroom. When he returned, it was Conrad's turn. Afterward, the two sat silently for an hour and a half before they were asked to return to the meeting.

"We have come to an agreement," Dixon announced. "The mill expansion has been completed, the strike and the riot are history and it's time to move on. I will recommend to BE&K's board of directors that it approve the agreement."

"The union will pay for damage to BE&K's property," Frank explained, "The amount will be less than what BE&K has claimed, but I will need to have the members approve a special dues assessment in order to satisfy the union's part of the bargain."

Frank and Dixon had done the heavy lifting. Jorgensen, who had never taken a case to trial, could continue to boast that he never lost before a jury. If Frank's special assessment were large enough, Ernie might be able to settle with Tyrone Gates and not have to explain Frank's leaflet to a jury.

"They had me over a barrel," Tyrone told his mother when he returned to the family home in Murfreesboro. He also had to tell her why he needed a pair of canes to steady himself.

"I'm no longer able to work and my disability checks weren't enough to live on. I was behind in my rent and utilities and could barely afford to eat."

His mother seemed smaller than he remembered. Her hair had gone from gray to white and her face had more wrinkles. She said she no longer took in laundry and was managing to get by on Social Security.

"I can't offer you much more than a roof over your head," she told him, "but you can stay as long as you want."

"I'll look for work," he said although he could think of no job that he'd be able to do and doubted that anyone would hire him in his condition. "Tell me about the tavern."

"When your father had his second heart attack he shuttered it," she said, "but he refused to put it up for sale. He thought he would recover and be able to reopen it like he did after his first attack. I pleaded with him to sell, but he was stubborn. The third heart attack finished him."

She asked about his injury and he told her about the riot.

"You said they stopped paying your disability benefits. Why was that?"

"My lawyer asked for my payroll records. That's how, Alderton Security found out about my lawsuit against the union."

"Shouldn't your lawyer have kept that to himself?"

"He had to tell Alderton why he needed the records. They had to know how much money I was losing. He said it was standard procedure. When Alderton learned that I settled my suit against the union, they stopped sending my disability checks."

"I don't see how that was a reason to stop sending your checks. What about your settlement? What happened to the money you got from the union?"

"After my lawyer took his share, he said the rest was up for grabs because the lawyers for the disability payments were claiming it. He said the law doesn't allow what he called 'double-dipping,' which meant I couldn't get disability payments and a union settlement, too. That stopped my checks and said I had to give back what they already paid me. My lawyer said they had a lien. When I asked hm what he was gonna do about it, he said it wasn't included in our retainer agreement. He told me I'd have to get another lawyer."

"Did you get another lawyer?"

"I tried, but the lawyers I went to wanted their money up front. It was way more than I could afford."

When she could think of nothing else to ask, he went upstairs to his old bedroom. It looked the same as it had before he left, only smaller. He sat on the bed for a few minutes and went downstairs again. The living room and kitchen seemed smaller, too. The whole house seemed smaller.

"Did you say you're not taking in laundry anymore?"

She nodded her head.

"I'll go to the bank tomorrow and ask if I can borrow some money to fix up the tavern."

"It needs a good scrubbing, but I don't know what else."

He didn't know if he was capable of managing a business that might keep him on his feet for hours. He also thought that if he reopened the bar, he might become a drunk like his father. He doubted that a bank would give him a loan, but telling her he would ask made her feel better. It even made him feel a little better.

Jack Ross slipped his sport jacket off, hung it on the coatrack in Lulu's Cafe and sat at the counter. While he waited for his coffee, he loosened his necktie, unbuttoned his shirt collar and folded the sleeves back to his elbows.

"You're the first one in this morning," Wanda said. "I put the pot on a while ago. It's fresh made. What has you up and about so early?"

She was wearing her usual outfit of tan slacks, blue blouse, white tennis shoes and an apron with freshly laundered stains.

"I drove up from Duluth yesterday and met with the other building trades before sitting down with the mill management."

"Stayed in town last night?" she asked.

"Yeah. I went to Benny's, too, and it wasn't easy getting up this morning. But I wanted to get an early start. It's still early isn't it?"

She set the coffeepot down.

"So, tell me. Is the mill in trouble? Is that why you're here?"

"I ain't supposed to say, but the whole town will know soon enough. There's gonna be layoffs, but the mill will keep operating."

"There's already been layoffs," she said. "What's going on?"

"There's gonna be more. The meeting was to see if the building trades can take in some of the mill's skilled workers after they're let go."

"And?"

"Fat chance. There ain't enough jobs for the members who are already signed up for work. It's the same story for most of the trades, not just my ironworkers."

Hank Peterson came in, hung his jacket and sat next to Jack.

"When did you drive up?" he asked.

"Yesterday."

"Stayed the night, huh?"

"I'll be on going home as soon as I finish my coffee."

Wanda grabbed the pot, set a cup in front of Hank and filled it.

"I'll have one'a those." Hank pointed.

When she returned with his glazed donut, she asked, "How's Mary?"

"Up all night again, but she was sleeping when I left. I needed to get out'a the house for a few hours. She'll sleep past noon."

"You need a hobby," Wanda said "something to take your mind off Mary."

"Now that I'm retired, I wouldn't mind some part-time work. Something in sales would be okay. I'd even be willing to work as a stock clerk, but local stores aren't hiring. They tell me business is slow."

"When I retire," Wanda said, "I won't even consider taking another job. I've had my fill of work. When are you gonna retire, Jack?"

"It might happen sooner than you think," he said. "I'm tired of delivering bad news. But, I've got good news for you, Hank.' "

"What's that?"

"BE&K settled with the labor board. There's gonna be back pay for folks that got fired or weren't hired because they were union. You'll be getting a share of that money."

"Any idea how much?"

"Not yet. The board's still figuring that out. But we should have an answer in a matter of weeks."

"I'll believe it when I see it, but thanks for telling me. What about Boise-Cascade? That's why you're here, ain't it? The rumor is there's to be more layoffs. I thought he expansion was supposed to create jobs. Why are people getting laid off?"

"The paper industry is in a slump," Jack said. "Companies are losing money. Blame it on foreign competition and a slowing economy. Mills are being bought by bean counters who close them or sell them to other bean counters for tax write-offs. Boise-Cascade will survive, but right now it's downsizing."

Lulu's weekday regulars began coming in the door. The few who were dressed smartly were business or professional people. Wanda, with coffee pot in hand, circulated among the tables and booths, chatting and taking breakfast orders.

"Time to hit the road," Jack announced. "I'll skip breakfast 'cause Edith will have lunch waiting."

"When will you be back?" Hank asked.

"Hard to say. There aren't any jobs for ironworkers, yet—not this early and this far north. There'll be work in the Cities before anything happens here or in Duluth. I'll be in touch as soon' as I hear from the labor board. Let me know if you hear something before I do."

Jack got up as Jerome came in and took his seat at the counter. Wanda asked Hank if he'd like to take something home for Mary. He shook his head.

"I'd like some coffee," Jerome said.

She got him a cup and poured.

Jerome had applied for a job at the mill and was waiting for a response. He was still living alone. His wife was living in Chicago and had filed for divorce. If he hoped to win her back, he would have to find steady work soon, preferably with a local employer. He knew it also would help if he quit drinking.

"Did Jack say anything about his meeting yesterday?" he asked.

Hank stood and reached for his wallet.

"He said there's gonna be more layoffs."

Damn," Jerome said. "Damn."

Chapter Thirty-one

Rachel greeted the mailman at the front door. Inside, she separated the bills from the junk before handing a familiar envelope to Ernie.

"It's like getting a subpoena," he complained as he slid his pen knife beneath the flap.

"If I have to listen to those tired speeches one more time, " she said, "I'll get a splitting headache, and you will have a crabby wife. I**'s** your subpoena, not mine**.** This year you are on your own."

In the spring, the ironworkers union hosts its annual, Upper Peninsula banquet honoring retirees for their years of service, congratulating new journeymen and welcome apprentices to the trade. This year would also bring new leadership.

"Where's your better half?" Frank asked when he greeted Ernie at the entrance to the banquet hall.

"She's at home avoiding a headache, but sends her regards. Show me to the bar."

Standing in a crowd of thirsty ironworkers, Ernie sipped his drink in anticipation of a long evening. He declined Frank's offer of a seat at the head table, choosing instead, to sit with the rank and file. Frank could share the honors with his successor and the rest of the executive board. With his scotch and soda in hand, Ernie was led to a table and was introduced to Roger Beaudre and several other ironworkers. They were drinking beer. Roger mixed his with tomato juice.

"What're you drinking counselor?" he asked.

"Brandy and water," Ernie lied.

In the Upper Peninsula, brandy is almost as popular as beer. Roger thought he caught a whiff of scotch, but he let it pass.

"Aren't you the lawyer that represented us when we were sued because of what happened at International Falls?"

"I'm the one."

"Why did you settle? Were you afraid of a trial?"

"A trial is alway a gamble. Sometimes it's better to accept a result you may not like, in order to avoid a result that could be worse."

"Maybe the guard deserved something for what happened to him," Roger allowed, " but we never should have paid a dime to the Rat. "

Ernie was about to excuse himself and finish his drink at the bar when someone began setting food on the table. Roger's plate had roast beef with green beans, mashed potatoes and gravy. Ernie didn't remember what he had ordered when he accepted the invitation. His heart sank when his plate was set in front of him. He despised Brussels sprouts and the fish was room temperature and bland. He reached for a biscuit and some butter. The biscuit was fresh and hot. He helped himself to another and left most of his meal untouched.

While dessert was being served, Frank introduced the union's new business manager. Buck stood for a round of applause and introduced the head table and a number of local government officials who were in the audience. A state legislator stepped forward and gave the stump speech he gave during every election cycle. The applause was sparse and brief. Remarks from a state senator drew a similar response. When Buck announced that the district's congressman was unable to attend due to a prior commitment, the applause was punctuated by cheers.

Buck congratulated the union's recent retirees and welcomed a dozen apprentices to journeyman status. Roger and Ernie stifled yawns. Frank was asked for a few parting remarks, and then it was over.

"Let me buy you one for old times sake," Frank said when he caught up with Ernie on his way out. "Show me where are you parked and you can follow me."

They drove to the Shamrock and were joined by others. Drinks were ordered and Ernie fielded more questions from Roger.

"There's not much else that I tell can you. If a jury had given BE&K everything it asked for in its complaint, it would have burdened the union substantially more than the settlement. As for Tyrone Gates, there was no limit to what a jury might have given him."

"But it was a wildcat strike,"Roger protested. "It wasn't supported by a union. It was never even brought up at a meeting of our union."

"The leaflet," Frank reminded him. "That's what got us in trouble."

"The trouble with the leaflet was let the Rat know we were coming," Buck declared. "That was a mistake. But now the Rat knows what will happen if it bids work in union country."

"I still think we shouldn't have settled." Roger insisted.

Ernie cut in: "Both sides can claim victory. Maybe the union paid more than it thought it should, but BEK got less than it it thought it deserved."

Ernie wished that someone would change the subject. Frank obliged by announcing that he intended begin his retirement with a fishing vacation on Lake Superior. Buck said that he was eager to begin introducing himself to contractors. As the union's new business manager, he intended to take a militant stance. Roger was going to join his ex-wife in a celebration of his son's birthday. Ernie let it be known that it was time for him to call it a night.

Outside, the sky was cloudless and the moon as full. There was little traffic as Ernie drove south on US 41. He wondered if Rachel would still be awake when he arrived home. When his high beams picked up two small lights moving slowly across the road, he braked to a stop. The lights disappeared, and he waited. When no more deer crossed in front of him, he moved forward, staying below the posted speed limit until he got to U.S. 2 and turned west, toward Escanaba.

He parked in his driveway. No lights were on in the house and the front door was locked. He felt in his pocket for his key and fumbled with the lock. Inside, he turned a hallway light on, crossed the living room and went upstairs to their bedroom. The bed was made and had not been slept in. He went downstairs and turned a light on in the kitchen. A note in her neat hand was on the table.

"Visiting mom and dad. Will be home tomorrow. I love you."

Made in the USA
Monee, IL
12 January 2023